For more than forty years,
Yearling has been the leading name
in classic and award-winning literature
for young readers.

Yearling books feature children's
favorite authors and characters,
providing dynamic stories of adventure,
humor, history, mystery, and fantasy.

Trust Yearling paperbacks to entertain,
inspire, and promote the love of reading
in all children.

OTHER YEARLING BOOKS
YOU WILL ENJOY

AKIKO ON THE PLANET SMOO, *Mark Crilley*

THE EGYPT GAME, *Zilpha Keatley Snyder*

HOLES, *Louis Sachar*

THE INK DRINKER, *Éric Sanvoisin*

FIDDLEBACK, *Elizabeth Honey*

THE GEEK CHRONICLES: MAXIE, ROSIE, AND EARL—
PARTNERS IN GRIME, *Barbara Park*

HOW TO EAT FRIED WORMS, *Thomas Rockwell*

ANASTASIA KRUPNIK, *Lois Lowry*

LUCY ROSE: HERE'S THE THING ABOUT ME, *Katy Kelly*

ISABEL OF THE WHALES, *Hester Velmans*

Happy Birthday, Hero!

1

Zoe Quinn

ILLUSTRATED BY BRIE SPANGLER

A YEARLING BOOK

Published by Yearling, an imprint of Random House Children's Books
a division of Random House, Inc., New York

Visit us on the Web! www.randomhouse.com/kids

Educators and librarians, for a variety of teaching tools, visit us at
www.randomhouse.com/teachers

Library of Congress Cataloging-in-Publication Data

Quinn, Zoe.
The caped sixth-grader. Happy Birthday, Hero! / by Zoe Quinn;
illustrated by Brie Spangler — 1st ed.
p. cm.
Summary: Just after her twelfth birthday, Zoe Richards, daughter of a police officer and a social activist, learns that her family tree holds an inheritance even more exciting.
ISBN 0-440-42079-2 (digest) — ISBN 0-385-90304-9 (Gibraltar library binding)
[1. Heroes—Fiction. 2. Grandfathers—Fiction. 3. Middle schools—Fiction.
4. Schools—Fiction.] I. Spangler, Brie, ill. II. Title.
PZ7.F457Cap 2006
[Fic]—dc22
2005016318

Printed in the United States of America

June 2006

10 9 8 7 6 5 4 3 2 1

FOR GRAMPY,
WHO LOVED A GOOD ADVENTURE

CHAPTER 1

"ZOE . . ."

I didn't look up. I *couldn't* look up. I knew it was rude, but I was on the second-to-last frame of the last page.

"Zoe . . ."

Last frame. Seven words, tops. Lightning Girl's got Frostbite right where she wants him and—

"Zoe Alexandra Richards!"

I tore my eyes away from the page. "Yes, Mom?"

My mother shook her head, but I knew she wasn't really angry. "I was asking you a question," she said patiently. "Would you like some orange juice?"

"Sure." I held out my glass while she poured orange juice into it. "Sorry I wasn't paying attention. But Frostbite—he's Lightning Girl's big-time nemesis, a major villain—he was about three seconds away from complete and total world domination.

See, he stole this super megaweapon from the Army of the World Republic, which he converted to a freeze ray. Actually, *he* didn't convert it. He *kidnapped* the chief scientist guy from the AWR headquarters and then held the point of a sharpened icicle to his *throat* and *forced* him to make the mechanical adjustments. I was right at the part where Frostbite had pointed the

megaweapon directly at the orphanage where Lightning Girl grew up. He was threatening to ice-ify the orphanage if the World Republic didn't turn over control of the universe to him immediately. Lightning Girl was about to utilize the forces of wind and rain to create the ultimate storm cloud. . . ."

"Wow," said Mom. "Sounds intense."

"It is." I shrugged, tracing the rim of my juice glass with my finger. "But it's all in a day's work for Lightning Girl."

Boy, was that ever the truth. Lightning Girl was definitely no stranger to danger. Villains, monsters, natural disasters—she never backed down from a threat, and she always came out the winner. But as far as I was concerned, the thing that made her truly heroic was the fact that she never pretended she wasn't scared. In fact, in issue #72 she actually came right out and admitted to Agent Stanford of the Bureau of Absolute Secret Information and Covert Knowledge that supercriminals and tidal waves and acid-spitting mutant cobras made her nervous. Knowing that Lightning Girl got freaked out by stuff like that just made her seem even braver.

Mom sat in the chair across from me. "So what else does Ms. Lightning do besides fight evildoers?"

"She recycles."

"I didn't realize recycling was a superpower."

"It's not. It's an environmental responsibility. And she donates to Greenpeace, and she never, *ever* uses aerosol hair spray—bad for the ozone."

"And bad for someone who works with lightning," Mom observed, sipping her coffee. "Highly flammable, that aerosol hair spray."

I nodded, giggling. "The point is Lightning Girl is a responsible superhero. She's totally socially conscious and passionate about what she believes in. Like you and me."

"And what exactly . . . ," came my father's cheerful voice from the kitchen doorway, "are my two favorite activists feeling passionate about today?" He stepped into the kitchen, pulling on his suit jacket. His badge was clipped to the breast pocket; the shiny metal caught a ray of sunlight and seemed to wink at me.

"Oh, the usual," said Mom, getting up and crossing the kitchen toward the fridge. "Animal rights," she said, opening the refrigerator door. "Civil rights . . ."

"And the most important right of all," Dad said. "The right to eat dessert for breakfast!"

Mom reached into the fridge and removed the biggest, most beautiful birthday cake I'd ever seen. It had bright green frosting and was covered with pink icing roses. I couldn't believe it. I'd been so absorbed in my comic book that I'd nearly forgotten what day it was.

"HAPPY TWELFTH BIRTHDAY!" said Mom.

"Thank you!" I grinned, suddenly feeling a whole 365 days older than the day before. "But could I take some for a recess snack instead? Then I can share it with Emily!"

"That sounds like a good idea," said Mom. She cut a couple of pieces and placed them in a plastic container. "There, now the roses won't get smushed on your way to school."

"Well, this is one gift you won't have to worry about smushing," said Dad. He reached into his pocket and pulled out a small box wrapped in shiny silver paper with pink and green ribbons. "Happy birthday, Zoe!" he said, handing me the package.

"Thanks!"

My mother slipped into the seat beside me to watch me unwrap the gift. Her eyes sparkled as I tore open the wrapping. The box was a perfect square of navy blue velvet. I opened the hinged lid and gasped. Attached to a velvet-covered piece of cardboard were the most amazing earrings I'd ever seen—two little gold lightning bolts, each with a tiny diamond chip shimmering at the tip.

"Oh, wow. Mom, Dad, these are so cool!"

"Turn them over," Mom suggested.

I gently slid the cardboard out of the box and immediately understood the reason for the sparkle in her eyes.

"They're for *pierced* ears!" I cried, and looked from one parent to the other, my eyes wide. "Does this mean you're actually going to let me get my ears pierced?"

Dad nodded. "A whole year ahead of schedule."

"Thank you!" I jumped up from my seat and threw my arms around Mom, then hugged Dad. "Oh, thank you, thank you, *thank you!*"

I couldn't believe it! I'd been begging to get my ears pierced since I was eight, but my parents had insisted I wait until I was thirteen. I was so desperate that I'd even organized a sit-in in the living room to protest the unfairness of the situation. My best friend, Emily Huang, sat with me, and even Howie Hunt, my next-door neighbor, came for a while (but I think that was only because he thought we'd be serving cookies). My mom had said she was impressed by my organizational skills and had praised my natural activist instincts, but she still hadn't budged on the age issue. So for four years I'd watched miserably as nearly all of my friends marched happily off to the mall to get two little holes punched into their earlobes, while I'd been forced to tough it out with clip-on or stick-on earrings, and even though Emily (who is quite possibly the most fashionable, style-conscious person in the world) swore to me that those were perfectly acceptable substitutes, I knew better.

And now, miraculously, my parents had seen the light. I was finally going to be allowed to get my ears pierced.

"When?" I asked eagerly. "Where?"

"Today after school," my mother replied, chuckling. "At the Piercing Post, in the mall."

I had to ask. "How come you're letting me get them done a year ahead of schedule? What changed your mind?"

"Actually," said Mom, getting up to pour some more coffee, "it was Grandpa Zack's idea."

"Grandpa Zack?" I blinked. "Get out!"

My grandfather was the greatest, but I couldn't imagine he'd care one way or the other about me getting my ears pierced.

"It's true," said Dad, accepting a steaming mug from Mom. "He convinced us that you deserved it. You know, as a reward for helping him in the store."

I had spent weekday mornings during both Christmas and February breaks behind the counter at my grandpa Zack's dry-cleaning store on Main Street. It never felt like a job because I really do like spending time with my grandfather; we have a way of making each other crack up over the silliest little things. I like meeting the other shop owners on the block—and the customers who come in panicking over salad-dressing stains on their best blouses or soup splatters on their favorite neckties. I had no idea what any of that could possibly have to do with getting my ears pierced, but

I sure wasn't going to argue! I started to daydream about buying earrings.

"I'll pick you up at school," Mom was saying.

My birthday celebration was cut short by the ringing of my father's cell phone. He flipped it open.

"Detective Richards here. Good morning, Captain Walker."

Dad's eyes turned serious as he listened to his boss. I glanced at my mother. She was still smiling, but I could see the slight shadow of worry in her eyes. She's proud of my father and always supportive of his work, but that doesn't mean she doesn't worry a little (or a lot) every time he walks out the door to do his job. I understand perfectly; I worry about him, too. As well as being totally proud of my dad for being a police officer, of course.

As a police detective, it's Dad's job to study crime scenes, track down clues, arrest suspects, and question, or *interrogate,* them until they confess. I know firsthand what a good interrogator Dad can be—whenever I go to a sleepover or the beach or pretty much anywhere, he asks me billions of questions about who'll be there and when I'll be home and stuff like that.

It's pretty neat, the way our family works. It's Dad's sworn duty to serve and protect by seeing to it that the laws of the community are upheld. Mom, on the other hand, is a big-time activist. She's involved with every nonprofit organization in town and fights against all kinds of injustices, which, as she always tells me, occasionally means taking a stand *against* rules or ideas that are less than fair and need changing. Both my parents do what they can to make the world a safer, happier place—Dad does it by enforcing laws, Mom does it by challenging them. Of course, it would be a bit weird if my dad

7

ever had to come and arrest my mom for chaining herself to a tree or something.

"Second Avenue and Bailey Street," Dad was saying into the phone. "Got it." He checked his watch. "I'll be there in twenty minutes."

He snapped the phone shut and grinned at my mother and me. "Duty calls," he said.

He says that a lot.

Then he ruffled my hair. "Better get moving, Birthday Girl," he said, "or you'll be late for school."

"Okay." I gathered up my books and my lunch bag and headed for the door. Mom threw me an apple for my breakfast, and somehow I managed to find a spare hand to grab it out of the air.

Dad kissed my mother's cheek.

"Be careful," she said.

She says that a lot.

And as the kitchen door closed behind me, I decided I was glad she did.

CHAPTER 2

EMILY was waiting for me at the end of the driveway.

As usual, she was dressed to perfection in a pink T-shirt and denim miniskirt, just right for the early fall weather.

"Happy birthday!" she cried, giving me a hug. Then she handed me a purple envelope with my name written in bubble letters across the front.

"Thanks."

I tore into the envelope and removed the card. *For My Best Friend on Her Birthday*, it read.

"The card's kinda corny," Emily admitted. "But look inside."

I opened the card. Inside was a gift certificate for my absolute favorite store on Earth—Connie's Cosmic Comic Shop. "Excellent!" I particularly appreciated it because Connie's store was most definitely *not* Emily's favorite place to shop.

"I knew you'd like it!" Emily took a step back and examined me carefully.

"What?" I asked.

"You are so twelve!" she announced, tossing her silky hair. "You're totally mature. You know, I think I can actually see the maturity in your eyes."

"Well, after today, you're going to see it in my ears, too."

Emily gave me a puzzled look that made me laugh.

"I'm getting my ears pierced!" I explained.

Emily's mouth dropped open. "Shut *up*!"

"Seriously! My mom and dad just told me. They even bought me pierced earrings, so I guess it's official."

"What happened to waiting until you turned thirteen?" she asked as we started walking toward school.

"They changed their minds," I explained. "My grandpa Zack talked them into it."

Emily grinned. "He's pretty cool, for an old guy."

I nodded, then listened as Emily told me about this pair of superfunky boots she'd seen in *Miz Thing* magazine.

"I asked my mom if I could buy them, but when she saw the price, she absolutely freaked!" Emily sighed; the fringy edges of her bobbed hair fluttered against her chin.

"When I'm R and F, I'll be able to buy everything I want! And whatever you want, too."

R&F was Emily's abbreviation for "rich and famous." She used the phrase so often that it needed an abbreviation. She'd been using it ever since we'd met in first grade. Emily's plan is to grow up to be rich and famous, and I've never doubted for one second that it will happen one day. Emily is smart and outgoing, not to mention gorgeous. She's got shiny coal-black

10

hair that's cut in a sleek bob to show off her dark eyes, and amazing bone structure. She's tiny on the outside, but she packs a lot of personality.

"Lightning Girl has glow-in-the-dark boots," I informed her.

She smiled. "Bet *they* cost a fortune!"

I don't know half as much about fashion as Emily does, and she's not all that into comic books. You'd think that would be a bummer between best buddies, but Emily and I simply combine our two interests to create a common one: Lightning Girl's extensive (and unexpected) wardrobe.

"Actually," I explained, "they were just ordinary boots until she got kidnapped by Dementizor . . ."

"Dementizor? Which one is he again?"

"He's a second-tier supervillain. Not as strong as Frostbite but way more dangerous than the Bloodboiler."

"Oh, *that* Dementizor."

"Dementizor kidnapped Lightning Girl and put her in his dungeon, which was protected by a nuclear-powered force field. She managed to escape, of course, and defeat Dementizor—"

"And," Emily interrupted, beaming, "she came out of it with fashionably radioactive footwear on top of it!"

"EXACTLY!"

Emily gave me a pretend-serious look. "Of course, it would be a complete fashion disaster for a girl to wear glow-in-the-dark boots before Labor Day. And she'd have to have a matching purse."

We arrived at Sweetbriar Middle School and headed up the walkway toward the front entrance.

Emily elbowed me and nodded toward Megan Talbot, one of the most popular eighth-grade girls. Megan was flirting with Dan Keller, one of the most popular eighth-grade boys. I could appreciate the symmetry in that. That sort of thing was definitely one of the differences between elementary school and junior high. Flirting was practically a competitive sport, and the popular kids were at national-league level.

Megan tore her attention away from Dan long enough to nod hello to Emily and me. I returned the greeting by giving Megan a quick smile, being sure to keep a casual air. Inside, though, I was turning somersaults. An acknowledgment from one of the eighth-grade in crowd! This was big.

Emily sensed it, too. "She wouldn't have bothered to nod to us if she didn't think we were cool," she whispered to me.

I motioned toward the school steps. "Speaking of cool . . . there's Josh."

Emily gave a little snort of laughter. "Try not to melt," she advised.

That wasn't going to be easy. This was Josh Devlin we were talking about. Joshua Everett Chandler Devlin. Green eyes, silky brown hair. Surfer. Soccer star. Math genius. And if that wasn't enough to bring him onto my radar, in third grade he circulated a petition to keep five hundred acres of rain forest from being destroyed. That was pretty much when I started doodling his name in the margins of all my notebooks.

I'd only meant to allow myself a quick glance to admire Josh's adorableness, but I guess I wasn't quick enough. He saw me looking at him and, to my shock, he actually waved. Or maybe he was swatting at a mosquito. Or shading his eyes from the sun. Maybe it was a muscle spasm.

"Did you see that?" I asked Emily.

"I totally saw that," said Emily, smiling from ear to ear. "Josh Devlin just waved at you!" She gave me a high five.

"Excuse me?" came a pleasant voice from behind us.

I turned and came face to face with a girl I'd never seen before. She was a little taller than Emily but not quite as tall as me. Her pale blond hair was stylishly cut—medium length and shaggy at the bottom. She had green eyes and perfect teeth, the kind you'd see in a toothpaste commercial. She was carrying a bulging paper bag that smelled delicious.

The girl gave me and Emily a big smile. "I'm Caitlin Abbott," she said, extending her hand to shake. "I'm new here. Today's my first day. I'm in 6D."

"Hey, so are we!" I grinned back and we shook hands.

If Caitlin was aware that Emily was studying her outfit—an expensive-looking linen peasant top and a denim skirt with a frayed hemline—she didn't show it. Instead, she motioned over her shoulder toward the street. "I've just come to Sweetbriar to live with my aunt Nina. That's her over there."

I glanced where Caitlin had pointed and saw a glamorous-looking woman standing beside a sleek little sports car. I tried to imagine my mom in a pair of leather pants like the ones Caitlin's aunt was wearing. Not in a million years!

"Have a stress-free and soul-soothing day, Caitlin," Nina called, blowing a kiss to her niece. Then she smiled at me; our eyes locked and I felt a strange shiver race down my spine. Before I could figure out what was spooking me, Aunt Nina slipped gracefully into the sports car and zoomed off.

I shook off the shiver and turned back to Caitlin. "I'm Zoe Richards. This is Emily Huang."

Caitlin held out her hand to Emily, but Emily didn't notice; she was too busy admiring Caitlin's knee-high boots.

I gave Emily a gentle nudge; Emily managed to pull her eyes away from the new girl's footwear and shake hands.

"Those boots are awesome! Where are you from, anyway? Because I'm sure I haven't seen those boots in any store in a fifty-mile radius of Sweetbriar!" Emily said knowingly.

"My aunt Nina picked these out for me. I don't really follow fashion all that much," Caitlin said as we walked up the school steps.

Emily turned a little pale. For her, fashion was practically an obsession. For instance, I knew that the denim skirt with a designer label that she was wearing today was her latest break-the-piggy-bank purchase—she had been saving for it for months. I looked down at my own faded jeans and yellow polo shirt. My zip-front sweater was pale lime green, which Emily had assured me would make my brown eyes look golden. I wasn't sure if it did or not, but the sweater was soft and comfortable. I liked it when fashion worked out that way.

Caitlin glanced down at her boots and then looked at Emily's feet. "Size five?"

Emily nodded.

"Me too," said Caitlin. "You can borrow these boots anytime you want."

"Really?"

The expression of joy and gratitude on Emily's face was so extreme that I had to laugh. "You just made a friend for life," I informed Caitlin.

She flashed another glowing smile. "Two friends for life, I hope."

"So what's in the bag?" I asked. I might not know as much as

Emily about fashion, but I definitely know about the delicious smell of home baking!

"Carob brownies," Caitlin replied. "My aunt baked them for the class. They're her specialty."

"Okay," I said, "I recognize the word *brownies*. But what's carob?"

"Carob tastes just like chocolate," Caitlin explained, "but it's way healthier. Aunt Nina's all about being healthy—she's a yoga teacher."

Mr. Diaz, my homeroom teacher, was standing on the front steps. "Morning, Zoe, Emily."

"Hi, Mr. Diaz." I motioned toward Caitlin. "This is Caitlin Abbott. She's new."

Caitlin shook Mr. Diaz's hand.

"Welcome to Sweetbriar Middle School. Girls, you're just in time to sign up to audition for the school play. The sheet is on my desk—"

Before he could finish, Emily let out a squeal of excitement. "Let's be the first ones to sign up!" She grabbed Caitlin by the arm and led her into the building. "Come on, Zoe!" Emily didn't bother to look back as she bolted down the hall.

"You'd better hurry if you want to catch up to Emily," Mr. Diaz advised.

I turned and headed into the school. I could see Emily and Caitlin at the far end of the corridor, just about to turn the corner. Caitlin was having a hard time keeping up with Emily.

I took a step . . .

And then another . . .

And then . . . I was standing right beside Emily at the door to Mr. Diaz's classroom!

15

Like, *instantly*!

But that was impossible. It was a long corridor, and I'd only taken two steps. . . . At least, I only *remembered* taking two steps.

And yet I'd caught up to them in a split second. Maybe less! That's how it felt, anyway—fast. Really . . . *fast*! Not to mention weird.

I shook my head, trying to clear it.

Okay, I must have been daydreaming about getting my ears pierced and just *forgot* I was walking—or sprinting—down the corridor.

That made sense. Kind of.

Emily grabbed my hand and tugged me straight to Mr. Diaz's desk. She printed her name in big block letters on the first line of the sign-up sheet. Caitlin signed her name neatly on the second line.

"Caitlin," Emily said as I stepped up to the desk to add my name to the list, "today's Zoe's birthday, and she's getting her ears pierced after school."

Caitlin opened her eyes wide. I noticed they were a really gorgeous green and shaped a bit like a cat's. "Cool. Happy birthday." She pushed her blond hair back to reveal her own earrings—shiny black oval stones set in sterling silver. "My aunt Nina gave these to me. She's says they're the perfect size and shape for my face."

Emily studied them for a moment, then said with total seriousness, "They do go very nicely with your nose."

Mr. Diaz walked in just then and my first school day as a fullfledged twelve-year-old began.

16

Since it was a weekday, the mall was practically empty when Mom and I got there. We took the escalator to the second floor and passed the sporting goods store, a high-tech gadget gallery, and a clothing store where the mannequins all wore neon-colored wigs cut in Mohawks.

"Emily loves that store," I said.

My mother raised her eyebrows at the strange dummies in their suede skirts and sequined T-shirts. "That figures."

When I saw the pink neon sign of the Piercing Post, I gulped. In all the years I'd been waiting to get my ears pierced, there was one thing I had purposely avoided thinking about: *pain*. C'mon—someone punching holes through your ears? That's got to hurt, hasn't it? I saw Emily have her ears done two years ago and noted every detail. For a start, that thing they use to shoot the earrings into your ears? They call it a *gun*. That should tell you something.

Suddenly, the whole thing seemed less like a fashion statement and more like punishment.

Mom must have seen the color draining from my cheeks, because she gave me an encouraging nudge toward the piercing salon.

"M-maybe there's a line," I stammered. "I wonder how long we'll have to wait. Maybe a long, long time . . ."

"Welcome," called the teenage girl behind the counter. "You're my first customer of the afternoon!" Her dyed-green hair was short; it reminded me of a lawn that needed to be mowed. I just hoped I wasn't her first customer ever.

"So much for a long wait," I mumbled.

Mom gently pushed me toward the counter. "Today is my daughter's twelfth birthday," she told the salesgirl. "We're celebrating by having her ears pierced! She's been dreaming of

17

this day for years and we're both very excited."

I groaned. Now I wasn't just terrified, I was mortified, too. Why do mothers always have to give people your life story? Like this girl cared that it was my birthday. She was a *professional* ear piercer, and she didn't look like the type to get emotionally involved.

The girl's name tag read DAISY. "How many holes?" she asked. My mother looked confused.

"Two," I answered, trying to hide the tremble in my voice.

"Two in each ear?"

"Heavens no," gasped Mom. "Just one."

"One?" said Daisy. "Fine. Which ear would you like it in?"

"Both ears," I said. "One hole in each ear."

"One hole per ear, huh?" Daisy, who had six earrings in her left ear, four in her right, and another in her nose, looked as though no one had ever requested that before. "Hmm. Interesting."

She went into the back room to get the piercing gun, and my mother shook her head. "Did you see that?" she whispered. "She had a tiny emerald stud in her nose!"

I managed a giggle. "Maybe it was just a sparkly booger."

Mom made a face. "Yuck."

When Daisy returned with the piercing gun, I climbed onto a high stool.

"We use gold-plated studs," she explained, "with hypo-allergenic posts."

"Does it hurt?" I asked warily. After all, she should be the expert, with more piercings than a sieve.

Daisy just smiled and uncapped a blue marker.

"One in each ear," Mom reminded her.

Daisy made a small blue dot on my left earlobe, then another on my right. "Those look even," she announced.

I squirmed as she loaded the earrings into the gun. "Ready?"

I shut my eyes and squeaked, "I guess."

"Here goes." Daisy pressed the trigger and the piercing gadget made a sound like a very powerful stapler. *Pop.* I waited for the pain, the agony. . . .

Nothing.

Not even a pinch. Instead, the popping sound was followed by a tiny *ping*.

I opened my eyes. The gold-plated stud had shot right out of the gun and landed on the glass countertop next to me.

"That's funny," said Daisy.

"What happened?"

"Well, the earring didn't go through your earlobe. It sort of . . . bounced off it."

I frowned. "Bounced off?"

"Maybe I didn't press the trigger hard enough." Daisy reloaded the earring into the gun and once again pressed it up to my ear. Again I heard the piercing gizmo make its popping sound, and again I felt nothing.

PING!

This time, the stud landed on the floor.

"Something must be wrong with this gun," said Daisy. "Don't worry, though. We've got another one."

She disappeared into the back room and returned with a new gun. She looked really determined now, and I felt even more nervous. She loaded, aimed, fired. . . .

POP.

PING.

Daisy shook her head. "I don't know why it's not working." She gave me a tight smile. "I'm sorry, the Piercing Post won't be able to serve your piercing needs today. Seeing as none of our guns seem to be working."

I felt bad for her and hoped she wouldn't get into trouble with her boss. "Do you know of

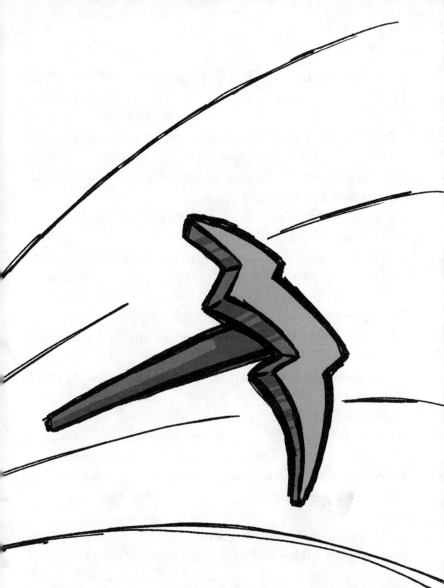

anywhere else that does ear piercing?" I asked as my mother helped me down from the stool. Now that I'd psyched myself up, I wanted to get it over with. After all, I really did want to have pierced ears!

21

"Well, there's Earrings 'R' Us on the first floor of the mall, and Hoop De-Doo's. You can also try Pierce-sonal Preference, The Stud Farm, and, of course, there's always Lobe-and-Be-Holed."

Mom frowned. "Do those places have stronger equipment?"

"I doubt it." Daisy gave an annoyed little sniff and held up the piercing gadget. "This happens to be the Stud Stamper 2000, the most powerful piercing gun on the market."

"Great," I grumbled. "Now what? We go down to the pier and borrow some fisherman's harpoon?"

"Don't be silly!" My mother patted my shoulder. "We'll try one of those other places another time, I promise. All of them, if we have to. But we're going to be late for dinner at Gran and Grandpa's if we don't get out of here."

I sighed. "But I wanted to wear earrings to my birthday dinner *tonight*."

"We have stick-on earrings," Daisy offered, pointing to a rack. "Sheets of ten. That's five pairs, if you're still committed to that one-in-each-ear thing."

I had to admit that some of the stick-on styles were cute, and since they didn't involve punching holes in my lobes, I could go wild and wear more than one on each ear. I picked out a sheet with stars, crescent moons, and even tiny yellow lightning bolts, without the diamond chips, of course.

As we left the Piercing Post, I could have sworn I heard Daisy muttering something about "granite earlobes," but I ignored it.

On the upside, I wasn't worried about the pain anymore. If the Stud Stamper 2000 didn't hurt me, I figured nothing could. And no way was I going to miss the chance to take advantage of Mom and Dad's letting me get them done a whole year ahead of schedule. Pierced ears, here I come!

CHAPTER 3

I ran up the walk to Gran and Grandpa's front door, partly because I was starving and excited about my birthday dinner, and partly because I just loved to run. I'd always been the fastest girl in my grade, and faster than most of the boys, too. When I put my mind to it, I could really bolt.

The door swung open. Grandpa Zack threw out his arms and caught me in a big, strong hug. "Happy birthday!" he cried, picking me right up off the floor. He was still pretty strong for his age, which was one of the things I loved about him. It felt like he wasn't much older than my dad. "Twelve years old! My goodness!"

"Happy birthday, Zoe, dear," called Gran from the kitchen.

My dad was already there; he was in the dining room setting the table. Mom went over and gave him a hug.

"Found this taped to the front door at home," said Dad, handing me a square purple envelope. He gave me a goofy grin. "My pro-fessional detective-like guess would be it's a birthday greeting."

I laughed as I took the card. "Ya think?"

"Who's it from?" asked Mom.

I had a pretty good idea. I opened the envelope and pulled out one of those warm-and-fuzzy birthday cards with a cute puppy and an even cuter kitten on the front, snuggling together in a flowerpot. When I read the signature inside, I couldn't help rolling my eyes.

"Well?" Mom prompted. "Who's it from?"

"Nobody," I said, tucking the card back into the envelope.

"Nobody who?" asked Dad.

"Nobody Howie, that's who."

Howie and I have been sending each other birthday cards since we were old enough to write our names. Dumb tradition, if you ask me—definitely not my idea. My mom is the one who makes me send cards to Howie, and I'm pretty sure his mom makes him send them to me, too.

But Mom was staring at the purple envelope with a weird misty look on her face.

"So, how did he sign it?" she asked in a singsong voice.

I shrugged. "Neatly."

My father chuckled.

"I mean," said Mom, "did he sign it, 'With Love, Howie'? Or just, 'Love, Howie'?"

"Eww. No!" I wrinkled my nose. "He just wrote his name—Howie Hunt. Neatly. In blue ink. Like he was putting his name on a book report or something."

Boy, did I want to get off *this* subject . . . and fast.

By now Grandpa was looking at me kind of funny; I guessed

he was staring at my ears, and I remembered that the whole ear-piercing thing had been his idea.

"Thanks for talking Mom and Dad into letting me get my ears pierced," I began.

For some reason, Grandpa looked disappointed. "No trouble at all."

I was about to explain that the actual piercing had been post-poned due to an equipment malfunction, but Mom told me to help get things ready for dinner.

In the kitchen, I paused to give Gran a kiss. "The lasagna smells great!" I said, grabbing a handful of cutlery and joining my dad in the dining room.

Gran knows lasagna is my favorite meal, especially when she uses my mom's recipe. They're always trading recipes and trying out new ones. Mom's a terrific cook, which she credits to being raised in a big Italian family where cooking and eating were considered art forms. I'm not much of a cook myself, but I've definitely inherited the eating gene. I could eat three whole helpings of lasagna and still have room for more.

"What's for dessert?" I called over my shoulder as I placed a butter knife on the tablecloth beside a plate.

"What do you think?" teased Gran. "Banana splits, made the Zoe Richards way!"

"With extra hot fudge! Excellent!"

A few minutes later, I was seated at the head of the table, where Grandpa had tied a dozen pink and green balloons to the back of the chair. He's done that every year since I was old enough to sit in a regular dining chair.

"Tell us, Zoe, dear," said Gran, sliding a square of lasagna onto my plate. "What did you do today?"

25

"Well, I broke the Stud Stamper 2000," I said.

Grandma gave me a strange look. "You broke *what*?"

"The Stud Stamper," I repeated. "The ear piercing gun. See? These are stick-ons." I tugged at my ears, to show her the adhesive stars.

"Stick-ons?" Grandpa repeated. "You mean those aren't pierced earrings?"

I shook my head. "For some weird reason, the piercing gun couldn't shoot the earring through my earlobe."

"That's peculiar," said Gran in a puzzled tone.

"THAT'S WONDERFUL!" cried Grandpa.

We all turned to look at him, and he cleared his throat.

"Uh . . . um, what I mean to say is that it's wonderful that you were at least able to get the stick-on ones. They look pretty real."

"But they're not," I grumbled, poking at a red pepper in my salad bowl. "We're going to try again tomorrow, but who knows if it'll work? It's like my ears are—oh, what's that word in the Lightning Girl comics? Indestructible."

Grandpa began to cough.

"Zachary, are you all right?" Gran asked, thumping on his back.

"I'm fine, I'm fine," he managed to say at last. "The lasagna was just piping hot, that's all." He took a long sip from his water glass and turned to me. "Indestructible, you say?"

I nodded. "Yes."

And suddenly I began to feel strange. Not bad or anything—but definitely strange. It started out as a tingle, like the feeling you get the night before Christmas or when the teacher is handing back a test you know you've aced—a feeling of excitement. But then the tingle changed to a crazy urge to get up, bolt out the front door, and start sprinting around the block at top speed. The feeling filled me until the tips of my toes seemed to vibrate inside my sneakers.

Run, my body demanded. *Run fast!*

My blood was pumping now, and my heart pounded like thunder. This was more than an urge. . . . It felt stronger than that. Much stronger. It was like a lightning bolt whizzing through me, and I found myself gripping the arms of the chair to force myself to stay in my seat. It wasn't as if I wanted to go run a few laps; it was as if I *needed* to.

"Zoe, are you okay?" Dad asked.

"I'm fine," I fibbed. "Just a little . . . antsy, I guess."

Somehow I managed to stay in my seat, but under the table, my feet were tapping like mad. When I glanced at my grandfather, he had this goofy smile on his face. I smiled back and tried to make my feet sit still.

And then suddenly the feeling stopped—went away, just like that.

I breathed deeply, easing my grip on the chair. Maybe all that tingling was a result of extreme hunger and I just needed to get some food into my system. That made sense.

I reached for my fork and dug in.

"Guess what Emily gave me," I said, swallowing my first bite of lasagna. "A gift certificate to Connie's Cosmic Comic Shop!"

"I know the place," said Grandpa. "It's right down the block from my store." He paused. "Connie's the one with the green hair?"

27

"Hot pink," I corrected him.

"My mistake."

"Connie's shop is the most awesome place!" I said. "Wall-to-wall comics, and comic-hero posters and comic-hero action figures, and Connie's like a walking encyclopedia of comic-book information. She knows everything about every comic-book hero ever drawn—Superman, Spider-Man, all of them! Well, except for Lightning Girl, but nobody in the whole wide world knows the full story of how Lightning Girl became a superhero. Of course, Connie doesn't call it Lightning Girl's story, she calls it her mythology, which sounds way more cool and mysterious, don't you think?"

One of the biggest disappointments of my life is that I have never actually read the first installment of Lightning Girl comics, or LG #1, as Connie refers to it. It's pretty much impossible to find a copy. There was a rumor that an anonymous collector paid over a million bucks for one, and it was believed to be the last copy in existence. Comic book experts said that even the woman who created the series, Electra Allbright, didn't have a copy of LG #1. And they said she'd vowed never to tell anybody, ever, what happened in that first comic book, but serious LG fans like Connie and me are committed to reading every new issue in an attempt to put the pieces together and figure out Lightning Girl's mythology for ourselves.

When I explained this, Dad laughed and rolled his eyes. "A vow, huh? Sounds more like a marketing strategy to me."

"I guess it is weird to keep a superhero's mythology so secret," I said, crunching into a chunk of garlic bread. "But it just adds to the excitement. The mystery."

"This is true," said Grandpa Zack. "Very, very true."

He sounded sort of serious and I wondered if maybe he was a bigger comic book fan than he'd ever let on.

"Eat up," said Grandma, passing me the Parmesan cheese. "Before it gets cold."

Through the rest of dinner, I had the weirdest feeling that Grandpa was looking at me. Not just looking at me, but *examining* me . . .

When the lasagna plates had been cleared away, Gran brought me an enormous banana split dripping with hot fudge and topped with twelve candles. When I blew out the candles, I wished for a fabulous thirteenth year full of happy surprises and good times. Oh, and to find out the secret of Lightning Girl's "mythology."

"How about we go out back and play a little catch? Work off some of that ice cream?" Grandpa suggested when we'd finished our desserts.

"Okay." I got up and headed for the back door.

Outside, the sky had gone soft and inky blue. It was that magical hour just before dusk when the world seems bathed in a special sort of light, and for a moment, a ray of fading sunlight surrounded Grandpa in such a way that I could have sworn he was actually . . . glowing.

"Okay, you go over there near the fence," Grandpa said, tossing the baseball from one hand to the other.

I slipped on the extra baseball glove I kept in my grandparents' garage and jogged toward the far edge of the lawn. At least, I meant to jog. My mind was thinking *jog*, but my feet seemed to have other plans, and the next thing I knew, I was running at top speed, skidding to a stop on the other side of the yard.

I wasn't even out of breath.

29

Before I could say anything, Grandpa threw the ball.

It was a lob, really, that arced up toward the darkening sky, then began to drop at about the center point of the lawn, far short of where I'd somehow ended up.

I knew the ball would hit the ground before I could get to it, but I decided to at least try to reach the middle of the yard before it landed in the grass.

THUNK!

I made the catch.

I MADE THE CATCH.

I made the catch because all of a sudden I wasn't at the far side of the yard, I was smack dab in the middle of it, under the ball.

But how?

I couldn't have run that far in less than a second! I was fast, but I wasn't *that* fast.

Or was I?

I blinked at the ball that had dropped squarely into the well-worn pocket of the old glove.

I looked at Grandpa; he didn't seem to notice anything miraculous about the catch, so I threw the ball back to him. Expecting another short toss, I stayed in the center of the yard.

But this time, Grandpa Zack hurled the ball with all his might. It whizzed past my head like a comet, sailing toward the fence.

And in the next second I was sailing toward the fence, too, passing the ball, and turning around to catch it easily, with seconds to spare.

"Whoa."

Grandpa laughed. "Whoa, indeed."

"Grandpa . . . ," I began, gulping. "Do you smell . . . smoke?"

Grandpa nodded toward my feet. I looked down and saw that my sneakers were smoking.

MY SNEAKERS WERE SMOKING!

"Okay," I yelped. "Either I had way too much hot fudge and I'm having sugar-induced hallucinations, or . . . or . . ."

Or what? I had no idea.

But judging from the way Grandpa was grinning at me, he had a pretty good idea.

"Zoe," he said calmly, "I have something to tell you."

CHAPTER 4

"**I**'m a *what?*"

I was sitting on the worktable in Grandpa Zack's garage, with my stocking feet dangling. Grandpa had unlaced my cross-trainers and held them up to inspect them. Their rubber treads had gone all gooey. "Melted," he had pronounced before tossing them in the trash. "Superspeed'll do that. It's the friction."

And he'd said it all so . . . *casually.* As though it were perfectly normal for a kid to run fast enough to liquefy the rubber soles of her shoes.

Then he said, "Congratulations, Zoe. You're a superhero now."

And that's when I said, "I'm a *what?*" My mouth hung open in shock.

"A SUPERHERO,"

Grandpa repeated.

"What, like Superman and Spider-Man?" I paused. "Like *Lightning Girl*?"

"Very much like Lightning Girl," he said, and the tone of his voice made me shiver.

"Yeah, right."

I stared at him, waiting for him to start cracking up.

He didn't.

So I did. I couldn't help it—I laughed so hard I was almost crying. After all, it was a pretty good joke when you thought about it. Did he really think I'd buy it? Did he really think I'd believe I was a superhero, with powers and everything?

"Zoe . . ." Grandpa pressed his lips together and shook his head.

I stopped laughing.

"Hang on a second!" I said, jumping off the worktable and squaring up to him in my socks. The concrete floor felt cold under my feet. "How do you *know*? That I'm a superhero, I mean?"

Grandpa held my gaze for what seemed like ages but was probably only a few seconds. I was so jangled up, I had totally lost track of time.

"Trust me," he said. "I know about this kind of stuff. You have powers," he continued in the same level tone, as if we were discussing a school project or last season's Little League results. "Special powers. Powers you are to use only for good works and unselfish deeds."

I stared at him for a good minute.

He was kidding me, of course. I wasn't a superhero! There was no such thing . . . was there? Okay, so my earlobes did break the most powerful earring gun made, and my sneakers did melt, and I was able to outrun a speeding baseball, but those things could be explained. Easily explained.

I just couldn't seem to come up with the explanations at that moment.

"I know it's difficult to believe, Zoe," he said, squeezing my shoulder. "But it's true."

"It can't be."

"But it is."

We were quiet for a very long time. Feeling kind of stunned and really confused, I gazed around the familiar garage. Grandpa and I spend lots of time in there together, and I recognized everything about it—the smell of old wood and motor oil; the damp chill that never went away, even in midsummer; the rakes and shovels and lawn chairs; and in the middle of it all, Gran's car, freshly waxed and gleaming in the light cast by a single bulb on an overhead chain.

The garage was the same as it's always been.

But suddenly I felt very, very different.

"You . . . you aren't kidding around, are you?"

Grandpa shook his head. I knew he was telling me the truth; he'd never looked so serious before.

"I really do have powers?"

He nodded.

I had to ask. "What *kind* of powers?"

Grandpa nodded toward the melted sneakers, still smoking in the trash can. "At present, I think we can safely say you've got superspeed. And the earlobe thing, well, you can chalk that up to the fact that you possess superstrength."

35

My eyes opened wide. "You mean I really am indestructible?"

Grandpa grinned. "Well, maybe not indestructible, but close."

Well, that could turn out to be exciting! I was suddenly picturing myself walking tightropes and scaling rocky cliffs. I could be the first kid at the town pool ever to attempt a triple reverse gainer with a half twist off the high dive . . . into an empty swimming pool!

Then I pictured myself toppling off the wall bars in third grade.

"I can't be indestructible," I challenged. "Remember when I was eight and I fell off the jungle gym and broke my wrist?"

Grandpa nodded. "Your superpowers hadn't shown themselves yet. They don't, generally speaking, until sometime after you turn twelve. Yours have come bang on schedule."

My voice was barely a whisper. "Why? And how do you know all this stuff?"

Grandpa took a deep breath and let it out slowly. "Let's start with your first question, which is a good one and one to which there is no single, simple answer." He paused. "You know your friend at the comic book shop? Connie?"

"Yeah."

"You told me she knows the mythology behind every superhero. Well, that's kind of the answer to your question. A superhero's mythology is really just the story, the facts behind how they came to be who they are, how their powers developed and why."

My mouth dropped open. "Grandpa, are you saying that *I* have a mythology?"

"Yes, Zoe, you do. And it will be revealed to you soon enough." He smiled gently at me, as if he were looking at me after a hard day of Little League. "But I think you've got enough to take in right now. For the moment, I can tell you this: you are what we call a Legacy Super. That means that you come by your powers genetically. Which brings me to your second question—how I know all this stuff."

I was floored. "You mean this superhero thing runs in the family?"

"That's right." He rubbed his chin thoughtfully and said, more to himself than to me, "Where to start?"

I was feeling more confused by the minute. "That must mean that I got these powers from Mom and Dad. Why didn't they tell me about any of this? I mean, this isn't the kind of thing you just spring on a person!" I began pacing the garage floor. "Oh, Zoe, happy birthday, have some lasagna, and by the way, one of these days you might be called upon to save the universe."

Grandpa chuckled. "Zoe, must you be so dramatic? No one is expecting you to save the universe . . . yet."

I didn't like the sound of that. "I can't believe you knew all along and never told me." I kept right on pacing. "And Mom and Dad never even dropped a hint!"

Grandpa shook his head. "They couldn't. Your mother and father know nothing about this."

I nearly tripped over a rusted watering can. "They don't *know*?" Now I was really confused. "But you said this is a genetic thing."

"I also said it was complex. Your father—my son—did not inherit the supergene."

We'd studied genetics a little bit back in fifth-grade science, and I struggled to remember what we'd learned. "So the supergene skips a generation?"

"Sometimes. Sometimes it skips two or three generations.

37

Sometimes five generations in a row will be Super. Sometimes the oldest and youngest siblings in a family won't be Super but the middle child will." Grandpa shrugged. "The process is completely unpredictable—there is no pattern to who gets the supergene. When it happens, it happens. And when it does, it's usually around the age of twelve, give or take a few months. So you see, I didn't know for certain that you would become a superhero. I only knew it was possible."

I was trying to keep up with all the information that was coming my way. "Okay, so this Super stuff skipped my dad's generation. But that means it would have had to skip *from* one generation to another—over his, right? Does that mean the super gene *didn't* skip your generation? *You're* a superhero, too?"

Grandpa slipped his hands into his pockets. "Well, that's sort of a tough question."

"How is that a tough question?" I demanded. "Either you are a superhero or you aren't! I am. Dad's not. And you . . . ?"

"I am a *retired* superhero," Grandpa explained. "Which means that for most of my life I was indeed an official, card-carrying, full-fledged superhero." He stood a little straighter, puffing out his chest and lifting his chin. "Zip, at your service."

I had to hold back a giggle. "Zip? Your name was *Zip*?"

"Perfectly appropriate, I assure you," said Grandpa, taking a key from a peg above the worktable. "In my day, I could zip around this little planet like nobody's business! Oh, I was fast!" He pinched my cheek. "You may have your grandma's sense of humor, kid, but you get your speed from me!"

He smiled and tousled my hair. "Zoe, think of it! You are about to embark on an entirely new kind of life."

As exciting as all this was, I wasn't sure I wanted a new kind of life. I was pretty attached to the one I had.

"But I like my old life," I said. "I mean, my present life. Sure, my parents can be a little overprotective sometimes, but I wouldn't trade them for the world. I've got Emily and school . . . and there's a school play coming up. Is everything going to have to change?"

It was completely overwhelming. Did superheroes get overwhelmed? Were they allowed to? Suddenly I didn't even feel as if I was twelve years old, let alone a superhero. Whatever that was supposed to feel like. And if I didn't know that, how could I possibly be one?

Grandpa put his arm around my shoulders and squeezed. "None of that will have to change. I promise."

"But you just said I'd be starting a new life!" I protested. I could feel my chin doing that annoying precrying quivering thing, and I really hoped that I wasn't about to have an attack of those really embarrassing crying hiccups.

"I meant a new *phase* in your life. Think of these powers as a special kind of talent you never knew you had. Being a superhero is, in the truest sense, part of who you already are: Zoe Richards. Nothing can ever change that."

I squirmed out of the hug and pulled back to look him in the eye. "So . . . like, I don't have to . . . I don't know . . . move away to some uncharted island where they train superheroes and find myself a sidekick? In LG number seventy-four, Lightning Girl went to training camp with Tornado Boy. It was on some tropical archipelago in the middle of the ocean, and Tornado Boy got a pretty bad sunburn."

Grandpa smiled. "There is no such island—not that I'm aware of, anyway. And as for having a sidekick, I hear they can be very handy for taking care of the small stuff, but you can decide later whether you want one or not."

I sniffed and felt the corners of my mouth tugging up in a grin. Grandpa hugged me again, and for a long moment, I let the incredible news sink in. I was a superhero. I had superspeed and superstrength. I felt a ripple of anticipation, a somersault of excitement in my stomach. *I was a superhero!* In the next instant, I had a million questions.

"Exactly how strong am I?"

Grandpa looked around the garage. "Well, let's see if you can lift that."

I followed his gaze to a large sledgehammer that he had leaned against the rear bumper of Gran's car.

"You want me to pick up the sledgehammer?"

"No, I want you to pick up the car."

I laughed. Grandpa didn't.

I stopped laughing. "You're serious?"

Grandpa nodded. "Go ahead. Give it a try. Just go slowly to start."

I went over to Gran's snazzy little powder blue car. I bent my knees and secured my fingers beneath the frame of the car, taking a deep breath.

With hardly any effort at all, the rear tires rose off the garage floor. Lifting the back of the car in the air, I passed it hand over hand until I was holding the *entire* car above my head!

Unfortunately, the sledgehammer that had been resting against the bumper fell on my foot.

I gasped, waiting for the pain to explode in my toes. But the pain didn't come.

"See?" said Grandpa. "That was a cinch."

"It was," I said, lowering the car to the floor. "And the hammer didn't hurt a bit."

"That's because you're as close to unbreakable as it's possible to be." Grandpa laughed. "Yessir, it would take an awful lot more than a measly sledgehammer—or an earring gun—to do *you* any damage!"

I felt such a rush of excitement that I began to hop around the garage.

"This is just *so* freaky! I mean, I just lifted a mint-condition 1965 Ford Mustang like it was a tricycle. I dropped a hammer on my foot, and look!" I shoved my foot toward Grandpa. "There's not even a bump! Don't you find it freaky, Grandpa?"

"Not especially," Grandpa answered, putting the hammer on the table and brushing off his hands. "When I turned twelve, my granny Zelda shot me out of a cannon."

He crossed the garage and unlocked the tall red metal chest in the corner—a chest I had always assumed held drill bits and screwdrivers.

"I must say, Zoe, lifting that car was very impressive. You seem to have a much better command of your emerging powers than most apprentice heroes. It took me weeks of practice before I could lift a car."

"Really?" I felt myself blushing. "Well, I guess I have always been sort of advanced. I mean, I did skip up to the seventh-grade math textbook this year."

Grandpa chuckled as he took an impressive-looking leather-bound scrapbook out of the chest. He handed the book to me.

I opened the cover and found pages and pages filled with newspaper clippings from something called the *Heroic Herald*, which seemed to be a sort of superhero newsletter.

41

"Grandpa, is this you?" I asked, trying not to laugh.

I pointed to a newsprint photo of a young superhero, cape flying in the wind as he hovered in midair to catch an enormous passenger train plunging off a cliff. There was another photo of the same handsome young hero holding up what I recognized from geography class as the leaning tower of Pisa.

Grandpa looked at the second photo and sighed happily at the memory. "Yes, that's me. I got there just in time to stop the thing from toppling over completely."

"Why didn't you stand it up straight?"

"I was all set to. But the people of Pisa decided they liked the angle, so they asked me to leave it that way."

I put the scrapbook on the worktable. "I'm guessing this superhero newsletter isn't something you can pick up at the local newsstand, huh?"

"It goes out monthly to members of the Superhero Federation," Grandpa explained. "As you might imagine, it's important for folks like us to keep a low profile."

"The whole secret identity thing," I said. I knew all about this from my comics—not that I'd ever imagined I'd have my own secret identity. Hang on, did that mean *Zoe Richards* was my secret identity? I shook my head and tried to figure out the whole hidden identity thing. "I guess ordinary people would have a tough time getting used to the idea of superheroes."

Grandpa looked serious. "It goes much deeper than that," he said softly. "Most people would be comforted to know that superheroes truly exist, that there are good, powerful forces looking out for the innocents in the world. But others . . . well, some would be angry and envious. Others might try to use superheroes to their own advantage. And others might become reckless."

"Reckless?"

"Well, Ordinaries might be tempted to do dangerous things, assuming a superhero will come along and save them." Grandpa held up his hands in a slow-down gesture. "But that's something we can talk about later."

That was fine with me. It was way too exciting being a superhero—*a superhero!*—to start worrying about the big stuff. I flicked through the album and found a color photo of my grandfather in his supersuit, silhouetted against a beautiful sunset. I shot him an approving grin. "Nice cape."

"Thank you."

I had reached the last page of the scrapbook. Pinned to the back cover was a large black and yellow patch, like a badge. "What's this?"

"This, my dear Zoe," said Grandpa, carefully unpinning the badge, "is the official symbol of your ancestry. It's our family crest, if you like." He handed the patch to me, and for a moment I got the feeling I was in some sort of ceremony—way, way more important than getting my level-one first-aid certificate (my mom made me take the course—she said you never know when you might need to perform the Heimlich maneuver—yuck!) or graduating from high school—or even getting a driver's license.

"You will be the latest in a long line of superheroes to wear it," Grandpa went on. "Of course, your own badge will be made especially for you by the Superhero Federation's uniform division—that same symbol in the colors you choose for your supersuit. Oh, and the Federation will choose an appropriate supertitle for you, once they've had a chance to observe your powers."

"They give me a supertitle? Awesome!" I sighed. "Too bad Lightning Girl's already taken."

"Yeah," Grandpa muttered. "That's too bad."

"And my own colors, huh?" I struck a pose. "Hmm. Is denim a color? I could be the first superhero ever to save the world in blue jeans! Nah, not denim. Too stiff. Okay, so what about maybe a faux leopard print? Or plaid. A nice pastel plaid!" My head was beginning to spin. I needed Emily here! After all, fashion was her specialty. She'd have me measured for something cool, clingy, and appropriately colored in no seconds flat.

I noticed Grandpa eyeing my socks. In honor of my birthday, I was wearing my all-time favorite pair—shocking pink and neon green stripes. "I guess I've always been partial to pink and green," I confessed. "Could they be my superhero colors, do you think?"

Grandpa nodded. "I think pink and green would be absolutely . . . super," he said, and grinned.

45

I hesitated, then held the black and yellow badge against the front of my T-shirt. We were both silent for a moment, then I asked, "How does it look? You know, if it were pink and green?"

"Perfect," Grandpa murmured, his eyes misty with pride. "Just perfect."

CHAPTER 5

I watched Grandpa unlock another drawer in the chest. It creaked as he pulled it open, as if it hadn't been opened in a very long time. I hoisted myself onto the worktable again and sat on my hands to stop myself from fidgeting. I had a million questions to ask him, maybe more, and I knew it was only a matter of time before Gran called us back into the house so I could open my birthday presents.

Grandpa removed another book, but this one was smaller than the scrapbook; it looked like the workbooks they give out in school, and it was tattered, with dog-eared pages as though it had seen a lot of use. He offered the book to me; I took it and read the title, which was printed across the front in plain black type:

SUPERHERO TRAINING MANUAL
BOOK ONE
Lessons 1–10
Apprenticeship

"That was the manual I used when I was in training," Grandpa explained. "All new superheroes get a copy. Er, I guess mine took quite a battering over the years." He grinned ruefully as I tried to smooth down some of the corners.

"No, it's cool," I said.

"I figure you can use it, too, though I'll need to find out if there've been any changes in the training since I studied. You'll begin as an apprentice hero, the level where you'll learn the most basic elements of being a superhero, including the rules, regulations, and guidelines of the Superhero Federation."

"Am I going to be tested on this stuff?" I joked.

"Absolutely."

I groaned. "Great. More homework."

"It will be worth it, I promise," Grandpa reassured me.

"So when do I start?"

Grandpa clapped his hands. "Immediately. That is to say, you can begin studying immediately. And I'm ready to begin your physical training whenever you're ready." I could tell he was trying not to sound pushy when he added, "The sooner the better, of course."

I scrunched an eyebrow down and grinned at him. "Like . . . tomorrow?"

"Tomorrow works for me!"

"Zoe," said Grandpa as we walked in the twilight back toward the house. "You must remember that this is a very big, very important secret."

"I get it, Grandpa," I said. "I won't tell anyone. Ever. Not even Emily."

Grandpa grinned. "Good girl. Not Emily, not any of the other children at school, not your mom and dad—"

"What?" I stopped in my tracks. This was not good. I had never been one of those kids who keep things from their parents. For one thing, my parents are very big on honesty. And for another, my dad is a detective! Knowing when someone isn't telling the whole story is one of his professional skills! And I am a lousy liar. For example, on the first day of kindergarten I accidentally broke the art teacher's green crayon; then I hid the pieces under a stack of construction paper. I would have totally gotten away with it, but the minute I got home, I confessed everything to my mom and dad, and the next day, I apologized to the teacher and replaced her busted crayon with the green one from my own brand-new box of sixty-four. And just recently I confessed to accidentally recording over my dad's videotape of the last game of the World Series.

"I don't want to lie to my parents," I said, surprised that my grandfather would even suggest such a thing. "Besides, you know how they are—they want to know where I am and what I'm doing every minute of the day! Even if I tried to fib to them, I'd never be able to pull it off! I have to tell them. I *want* to tell them!"

"You can't tell your parents," Grandpa said firmly. "They're non-Super, what we call Ordinaries." Grandpa pointed to the manual. "You'll find it in there, chapter two, section five A: 'Superfolk must not tell Ordinaries about their powers unless security clearance is granted by the Federation.'" He paused. "Actually, it might be section six B, but the point is you can't tell your parents."

I frowned. "I'm not cool with that at all." Mom and Dad may be a bit overprotective at times, but I could totally see the sense in telling them everything, especially where I was going and when I'd be back.

Suddenly my activist nature kicked in. "I'll start a petition to change that rule. Like the time I petitioned the Sweetbriar Wilderness Scouts to allow girls to join the troop. All I had to do was point out to the Wilderness Scout leaders that it was a dumb rule and—"

Grandpa gave a patient sigh. "No petitions, Zoe."

I frowned. "But Mom always taught me to stand up for what I believe is right. To challenge injustice and oppression."

"This isn't oppression," Grandpa Zack said. "It's plain common sense."

I considered his point. Okay, I could understand not letting my school friends in on it, but my family? How could I possibly hide the fact that I was a *superhero* from my mom and dad? And why would I want to? Wouldn't they think it was neat? "But Grandpa, they'd be really proud of me. I bet they'd take pictures of me in my superhero uniform—or whatever—and tell all their friends, maybe throw me a good-luck-as-a-superhero party and have a street in town named after me. . . ."

Grandpa raised an eyebrow but didn't say anything. Oh . . . hang on . . . now I understood. Grandpa was right. I couldn't tell my parents. If they knew about it, then it would be a secret they'd have to keep, too.

Grandpa put his arm around my shoulders. "Honey, this is one of the most difficult parts of the superhero life. I know that you've been taught never to keep secrets from your parents, and rightly so. The superhero secret is the one and only exception to that rule. For the good of planet Earth."

"What about Gran? Is she an Ordinary? Does she know you're a Super?"

"Yes to both," said Grandpa. "But your gran wasn't given a security upgrade until we'd been married for years. I tried to keep the whole thing secret from her. But my Sally is a very wise woman, and you can't hide much from her. She began to notice things, like the time I returned from the cosmos with stardust in my hair."

I stared at him in astonishment. "You went to outer space?"

"Only once. There was this giant meteor on a high-speed collision course with Bora-Bora. I was sent to catch it and hurl it back into deep space."

"How did you get there? With your superspeed? Did you have a ship?"

Grandpa looked uncomfortable. "Not exactly. I had a partner for that particular mission. Another superhero—one who had access to an interuniverse mode of transportation." He cleared his throat. "But that's not the point of the story. The point is that Gran put two and two together and figured out that there was no way I'd been out bowling, which was what I'd told her. I went to the Federation, made a formal request, filled out the paperwork, and two weeks later, I was able to tell your grandma everything."

"So if someday Mom and Dad suspect that I've got superpowers, I can tell them the truth?"

Grandpa smiled. "Let's cross that galaxy when we come to it, all right?"

"All right."

"I want you to read the first ten pages of the manual tonight," he instructed. "Then meet me at the dry-cleaning store tomorrow after school, to work on your superspeed."

Now, *that* sounded like fun. "Okay."

We'd reached the kitchen door. Grandpa put his hand on the doorknob, then turned back to me.

"Oh, and one more thing," he said with a wink.

"What?"

"Wear stronger sneakers!"

CHAPTER

6

I didn't say much on the ride home.

I sat in the backseat with my teeth clamped tightly together to keep from blurting out the mind-blowing news. I, Zoe Richards, was a superhero! *I* was a superhero! A *superhero*! I wanted to roll down the car windows and scream it to the world. At the very least, I wanted to tell Mom and Dad.

But keeping it a secret was a superhero rule, and there was no way I was going to break *any* of the rules, not when I'd only just found out about them. Every so often, I peered into the over-sized shopping bag that contained my haul of birthday gifts in their unwrapped boxes. The superhero training manual was safely hidden beneath the new pink fleece hoodie my parents had bought me.

When Dad pulled into the driveway, I grabbed the bag, bounced out of the car, and headed up the front walk.

"Uh . . . Zoe?"

I turned. "Yes, Mom?"

"Where are your sneakers?"

My eyes shot down to my feet, and I stared at the toes of my pink and green striped socks. "Oh . . . um . . . I left them at Gran and Grandpa's house."

"Why did you do that?" asked my dad in surprise.

"I . . . I . . ." I willed my brain to come up with a good fib. "I stepped in something gross! A big stinky pile of—"

"Say no more!" Mom wrinkled her nose. "I get the picture."

Upstairs, I checked my e-mail for happy-birthday messages— hey, even apprentice superheroes need to know their friends haven't forgotten their birthday—and changed into my pajamas before hopping into bed with the superhero training manual. I tried to imagine my grandfather at my age sitting down to study this very same book for the first time. And his granny Zelda before him, and before her . . . who knows? I felt as if every one of my superancestors were putting their trust in me. I opened to the introduction.

Congratulations, Hero!

If you have found yourself in possession of this most worthy of guidebooks, then it is certain that you have recently come into your superpowers. You are about to enter the apprentice phase of your superhero journey! Go bravely, go boldly, and may the forces of justice be ever present on your quest.

I felt a shiver. This was way official, not to mention a little poetic. I turned the page.

Before you read further, it is imperative that you understand, memorize, and recite the Pledge of Secrecy. You shall speak the pledge aloud just this once, for when you speak these words, they shall become one with the universe, part of the everlasting truth, binding you to the Federation for all time. Remember, this is your first duty: tell no one of your powers. Ever. Intone this pledge in a secure and secluded location where you will not be overheard. Do not delay. Do it now.

The Pledge of Secrecy

I, *[state your full name]*, do solemnly vow never to reveal to any Ordinary that I am a superhero. I shall endeavor to be stealthy, surreptitious, discreet, prudent, clever, cunning, and resourceful. On my honor, in the name of all that is Super, I promise to exercise due diligence in concealing my heroic identity and the identities of my fellow Supers from this day forward.

Surreptitious? Due diligence? Was this a superhero pledge or a vocabulary test? I went to the bookshelf over my desk, grabbed the dictionary, and looked up some of the bigger words, just to make sure I knew what they meant. (Mr. Diaz would have been so proud! Except, of course, he'll never know, seeing as he's an Ordinary and I'm a Super. A *Super*! Sheesh, I didn't think I'd ever get tired of saying that!) Once I understood pretty much what the pledge was all about, I read it over silently, again and again, until I had committed the entire thing to memory.

DO NOT DELAY. DO IT NOW.

I needed a secure location, and I needed one fast.

My first thought was to duck into my closet and recite the pledge in there, but when I opened the door, I frowned. The floor was a total mess, with piles of stuffed animals, board games, my ice skates, a tennis racquet, a few old dance recital costumes, and a pair of ski boots that hadn't fit me in years. I closed the door, hoping there wasn't some Superhero code of tidiness I was expected to follow. Speed, strength, and secrecy I could handle (I hoped); keeping my closet in order was a whole different matter.

I tucked the manual under my shirt and tiptoed out into the hall. My parents' bedroom door was open; I saw my mom sitting up in bed reading, and I could hear my father gargling in their bathroom.

As quietly as possible, I made my way downstairs and into the kitchen, remembering to step over the creaky floorboard in the hall. I wasn't sure whether superpowers could do anything about the noises from old wooden floors. The digital clock on the oven display panel threw off a weak green glow, lighting my way to the pantry. I opened the door, slipped in, and closed the door behind me.

I knew Mom's emergency flashlight was right on the second

shelf. I snapped it on, then removed the manual from inside my pj's.

I placed my right hand on the cover of the book and took a deep breath.

"I, Zoe Alexandra Richards, do solemnly vow . . ."

There in the darkness, I made my promise out loud, and the words I spoke filled the small space of the pantry, mingling with the smells of cinnamon bread, cocoa powder, and ripening tomatoes, becoming one with the universe.

". . . from this day forward," I finished.

The pantry, the kitchen, the entire universe, it seemed, fell silent.

It was just *too* cool. I'd made a promise to the whole world, and now the whole world was counting on me . . . even if the whole world didn't exactly know it.

I grabbed a handful of Oreos, put the flashlight back on its shelf, and went back upstairs to read some more.

CHAPTER

7

SUPERHERO TRAINING MANUAL
BOOK ONE
Chapter One
Section 3 (b)

Apprentice-level heroes are considered "in training" and are *not* authorized to perform superhero duties with regard to crime, natural disasters, or villains. For reasons of public and personal safety, superpowers must not be utilized by the apprentice until the first examination has been taken.

WARNING: *Powers at this stage of development can be volatile and may activate for brief periods with no voluntary action by the apprentice.*

> In the event that an apprentice does witness a criminal action or other dangerous occurrence, the apprentice should, like any good citizen, dial 911 immediately and alert the proper authorities.

Well, heck! That seemed like a rip-off to me. I wanted to use my powers as soon as possible! Not that I wanted anyone to be in danger just so I could do my thing. But if someone was in danger, it was going to be awfully hard to keep from rushing to the rescue.

But rules were rules. And I was going to do everything by the book.

At least I was going to try.

Believe it or not, I was late for school.

Me, the fastest sixth grader in the universe . . . late!

And the crazy thing was that it was my superspeed that made me late.

I got up on time, took a not-too-long-but-not-too-short shower, spent the usual amount of time picking out my clothes and getting dressed, then went downstairs and had breakfast at a perfectly normal, human pace.

Unfortunately, I dropped the toast. And even more unfortunately, the toast was slathered with strawberry jam. And most unfortunately of all, it landed jam side down in my lap.

"Oops."

Dad smiled. "Looks like you've gotten yourself into a sticky situation."

I peeled the toast from my lap and frowned at the gooey smear across the bottom of my T-shirt. "I guess I have to change."

"I'd say so," said Mom, taking the ruined toast from me and tossing it into the trash. "Run upstairs and put on something else. But hurry."

Hurry.

Well, what could it hurt? All I had to do was turn on a little speed. I knew it was against the apprentice superhero rules, but if there was one thing I'd learned from my mom, it was that sometimes you had to bend the rules a little to prove they were unfair. And maybe this particular rule didn't even apply to me. After all, Grandpa had said I had a good command of my powers. Surely the rules didn't apply to apprentices who happened to be superadvanced?

And anyway, it wasn't like I was gonna get caught.

I closed my eyes and focused all my energy on my feet until I could actually feel the power pulsing through my toes, toward my arches, and up my shins. The sheer force of it surprised me, and I gasped.

"Zoe, are you all right?"

"Fine," I said, bounding out of my chair. "I'll . . . hurry."

Gritting my teeth, I managed to make my feet walk out of the kitchen, but the second I turned the corner into the hallway, I was running.

Running fast, then faster, then at superspeed, up the stairs, down the hall, and into my bedroom.

So much for turning on a *little* speed.

"Slow down," I told my feet. "Just a bit. Please."

But they were having none of it. I hurdled the bed like an Olympic track star and bolted for the closet. Then my arms decided to get into the act. They banged open the closet door and began riffling through the clothes inside. The air buzzed as it was stirred up by the propeller motion of my hands and arms and shoulders. The hangers rattled loudly on the pole as I tugged clothes out and flung them around the room.

Pants, shirts, sweaters, jeans . . .

FLING, FLING, FLING, FLING . . .

The room became a blur of khaki and cotton, satin and suede. I couldn't stop. And the weird thing was, if I'd been moving at regular speed, I'd have already picked out an outfit, put it on, and left for school.

But my arms kept churning through my wardrobe until there was nothing left but a totally ugly ruffled blouse and an itchy-beyond-belief tweed jumper, both of which I'd hidden way back in the closet in the hopes that my mom would forget I owned them.

"Zoe," came my mother's voice up the stairs. "Can you pick up the pace a little?"

Ha! If she only knew!

I peeled off my sticky shirt and undid my jeans so fast that the zipper threw off sparks. Taking a deep breath, I forced my arms to slow down so that I could rummage through the heap of clothes on the floor and pick out something wearable; there was no way I was going to let my superspeed fling me into the ruffled blouse and the itchy jumper. I reached for a long-sleeved T-shirt. Moving slowly actually hurt!

"Zoe!"

Startled, I lost my concentration for a second and blinked—and by the time I'd opened my eyes again, I was wearing the T-shirt and a pair of khaki pants. Oh well, at least I'd avoided the itchy tweed.

"You ready, hon?" Mom poked her head around the door. Her eyebrows practically vanished into her hair when she saw the state of my room. Okay, so I'm never *super*tidy, but this was bad, even for me.

"What in the world happened here?"

"Well." I gulped. "You told me to hurry."

Mom narrowed her eyes. "Pick it up. Every single thing."

"But, Mom . . ."

"Zoe, you are not leaving this house until every article of clothing is returned to its hanger."

"But Emily will be waiting!"

"I'll tell her to go on without you."

"I'll get a tardy slip."

Mom folded her arms. "You should have thought of that before you ransacked your closet."

I did think of it, I thought sulkily. *I just couldn't do anything about it.*

Mom closed the door, stamped down the hall, and went back downstairs. I picked up a pair of black pants and folded them over a hanger. Then a pink turtleneck, then a striped cardigan . . .

Where was my superspeed now? I tried to kick it in, turn it on, dial it up . . . but nothing happened. The cleanup took me half an hour. It would have taken longer, but eventually I gave up and just shoved whatever was left on the floor under the bed, crossing my fingers that Mom wouldn't choose today for a spring clean.

When I got downstairs, Mom looked me over. "Very nice," she said. "Don't forget your coat."

I frowned. "Mom, it's warm outside."

"I don't want you to catch cold." She handed me my winter jacket.

"Mom! I'm going to school, not climbing Mount Everest."

She thought it over, put the heavy jacket back into the closet, then handed me a lightweight Windbreaker. "Zip it way up," she cautioned. "It might get breezy."

Arguing would only make me later, so I zipped the jacket all the way to my chin and got out of there before she could talk me into wearing mittens.

I arrived at school just in time for a tardy slip. As the principal's secretary wrote out my late pass, she commented on how this was not a great start to the new year, and how I should really try to move a little faster now that I was in sixth grade and everything.

It was going to be a very long day.

Mr. Diaz was standing in the hallway outside the classroom, checking his watch. "This isn't like you, Zoe," he said.

"I had a rough morning," I said. For a moment, I was tempted to tell him it was all because of being an apprentice superhero, just to see what he'd say, but then I figured I was already in enough trouble and shut my mouth again.

"Well, you've already missed the start of the spelling quiz," said

Mr. Diaz. "You'll have to make it up at lunchtime."

I followed him into the classroom, where everyone else had their heads down over the quiz. Emily glanced up and rolled her eyes sympathetically. I just shrugged, wondering if I should make up an excuse for being mega-late. And then I wondered just how many lies I would have to tell because of my superpowers. Superfibs weren't exactly what I had planned for my new life as a hero, that's for sure.

"You have three minutes remaining," Mr. Diaz informed the class.

While everyone else finished the quiz and passed their papers to the front, I rested my chin on my hand. *Maybe once I get my powers under control, I won't have to go to school anymore. Maybe there's some awesome private academy for school-age superheroes like me, where they never give spelling tests and the only subject is superhero PE.*

I imagined a gymnasium filled with sixth-grade superheroes. I could just picture them—us—all leaping easily from one end of the gym to the other, our capes flying, our tights shimmering. No need to lie if we were late due to uncontrollable powers, no dumb spelling quizzes—unless maybe you had to learn how to spell the names of all the different countries in the world, in case you were sent there on a mission. . . .

My fantasy was cut short by Mr. Diaz's voice. "Please take out your social studies textbooks and turn to page twenty-eight."

With a sigh, I reached into my desk, took out my social studies book, and turned to page twenty-eight, just like everybody else.

CHAPTER 8

AT lunchtime, Mr. Diaz gave me the spelling test. It took me a moment to recall whether *discombobulated* had one *m* or two. If X-ray vision had been one of my powers, I could have turned my eyes to the enormous dictionary on the bookshelf, X-rayed through the cover, and simply looked up *discombobulated* right from my desk. But that would have been cheating. And I was no cheater. Not that it actually mattered, because I didn't have X-ray vision . . . not yet, anyway.

I settled on one *m* and handed in my paper.

I got my lunch out of my locker and headed for my and Emily's favorite picnic table at the edge of the playground.

Emily was already there. Barbecue potato chips and a tuna sandwich sat untouched in the center of the table; she was busily shuffling through several piles of paper.

"What have you got there?" I asked, putting down my peanut

butter bagel and swinging my legs over the bench. *Slowly.*

"Only the world's most wonderfully tragic theatrical piece," Emily explained, looking up with a dreamy expression on her face. "Namely, *Romeo and Juliet* by Mr. William Shakespeare. Mr. Diaz said we could use whatever lines we wanted for the tryout. Auditions for the school play are this afternoon, remember?"

I stared at her in dismay. I hadn't remembered. And what was worse, I wasn't going to be able to go. I had a training session scheduled for today. And as this morning's episode had demonstrated, I needed all the training sessions I could get. But I'd promised Emily weeks ago that I'd audition for the play with her, even though acting isn't my thing. What was I going to tell her?

"I came prepared," Emily went on, obviously missing the look of panic on my face. Flipping through the pages, she flourished one with glee. "I printed off a bunch of the most dramatic scenes ever from the Internet. I'm using the famous balcony scene! I memorized these lines last night. I'll be okay as long as I can keep a straight face during that 'wherefore art thou' stuff. And I've already talked good old Howie Hunt into reading Romeo's part."

I glanced across the playground at "good old Howie Hunt" and was surprised to see that he was actually playing tetherball with Caitlin Abbott. Howie rarely got invited to play tetherball—or any sport—because he wasn't much of an athlete. I watched as the ball came swinging toward him; he swatted at it but totally misjudged the distance. With a loud *ping,* the rope wound around him, binding him to the tetherball pole.

"Howie Hunt as Romeo, huh?" I shrugged. "Is that what they call casting against type?"

Emily sighed, watching as Caitlin hurried to Howie's rescue. "He wasn't my first choice," she admitted.

"Bet I know who *was* your first choice." I grinned, lowering my voice to a whisper. "Josh Devlin, right?"

"Who *wouldn't* want Josh to be their leading man?" Emily swooned. "Josh is the coolest boy in the whole school. And he's a seventh grader." She gave me a wink. "But as I recall, he waved to you yesterday, not me."

Something went fizz inside me, but I told myself there was no way I was getting my hopes up over Josh Devlin. "Maybe he thought I was somebody else."

Emily rolled her eyes. I should have known I couldn't hide that fizz from her.

Okay, fine, so I had a crush on the guy. (There, I'd admitted it!) A major, big-time, doodle-his-name-all-over-my-notebook type of crush. It wasn't just because of his terrific looks. Josh is way sweet, and funny and smart. And he petitions! Against injustice and world oppression! Hmm, wonder what he thinks of superheroes. . . .

"Anyway," Emily was saying, "what are you going to read at the audition?"

I felt my stomach flip, and this time it didn't have anything to do with Josh Devlin. I couldn't possibly stay after school for try-outs today. And once I got the hang of my powers, who knew how much of my time would be taken up with superhero missions?

"Yeah. . . ." I bit my lip. "Um . . . about the play . . ."

Emily leafed through the pages and thrust one at me. It looked suspiciously like a musical score. "You could try something from *Annie.*"

"I can't read from *Annie!*"

"You're right. You'd need a curly red wig." Emily snatched the page back and handed me a different one. "How about *The Sound of Music*? It's a classic."

"Em, I can't do it."

"Sure you can. The scene where Maria makes the kids wear the curtains? Humor, drama, a song—it's totally your thing."

Pausing only briefly to wonder if Emily really saw my life as some sort of musical comedy-drama, I sighed and tried to look like I was concentrating on my lunch. "I mean, I can't even go to the auditions. I have . . . an appointment." *Superlie number one.*

I glanced up to see Emily looking utterly crushed. "What, like a dentist appointment? Or an appointment for a haircut?" Her expression turned from crushed to interested. "'Cause if you're getting your hair done, I think you'd look totally cute with some highlights. Yeah, some reddish highlights, and maybe some wispy layers—"

Before Emily could get too carried away with her hairstyle advice, I interrupted. "I've got to meet my grandpa Zack. At his dry-cleaning store." *Well, that wasn't a lie. Not even a super one.*

Emily groaned. "Please tell me you didn't stain that cool sweater I loaned you."

"No," I said. "I'm going to help out again, like I did over winter break. He needs help in the store, and he's asked me to come in after school until he can hire someone full-time." I wriggled uncomfortably. However important it was not to divulge my supersecret, there was nothing super about lying to my best friend.

Emily went back to looking crushed. "I was really hoping we'd both be in the play. I wanted us to be acting buddies."

"I could be your acting buddy," said a voice.

I looked up to see Caitlin standing beside our table, smiling and looking very sincere.

"I know I wouldn't be the same as a best friend like Zoe," she added, turning the beam on me, "but it still might be fun."

Pushing away the thought that Caitlin looked like she was aiming for an audition for a toothpaste commercial, I brightened as an idea took shape in my mind. "That's great!" I told Emily. "Caitlin will be a great acting buddy! And maybe, depending on how many missions—I mean, *hours,* I have to put in at the dry-cleaning store, I can be part of the backstage crew." I knew that helping out with sets and lighting wouldn't take up as much time as rehearsing and memorizing lines. If I joined the set crew, I could be part of the production and still have time to practice my superhero stuff.

Emily nodded as if this idea was just the right side of acceptable.

"By the way, Caitlin," I said, "it was really nice of you to play tetherball with Howie."

Emily giggled. "It was even nicer of you to untie him from the pole."

"He looked kind of lonely," said Caitlin, taking a seat across the table from me. She opened her lunch bag and pulled out a rather unappetizing-looking sandwich. The bread was the extra-healthy multigrain kind that looked like cardboard with sawdust stuck to it, and as far as I could tell, there wasn't anything between the two slices but bean sprouts.

I took a bite of my bagel as Emily and Caitlin discussed the audition and, despite a tiny pang of envy (being acting buddies did sound like fun), I felt very mature for not letting it bother

71

me that my best friend would be spending so much time with Caitlin. The year before, Emily had taken a Saturday pottery class (which I couldn't join because I'd still been suffering through piano lessons), and I felt jealous when, after two hours of squishing mud on the potter's wheel, she would go out for sodas with her classmates. I'd see Emily and the pottery crowd as they passed by the music school window with clay in their hair, laughing and comparing the lopsided vases they'd made, and I'd feel completely left out.

But then Emily had given me the vase she'd made as a Christmas gift with a card that said *To my best friend,* and I'd understood that true friendship couldn't be destroyed by a few measly Saturdays apart.

Besides, I had the superhero thing now. It was going to have to become what my parents would call a priority in my life.

Well, at least it would have to be more fun than piano lessons.

CHAPTER

THE afternoon seemed to last light-years.

I kept glancing at the clock. I couldn't keep my mind on the history lesson, or the grammar lesson, or the math lesson.

All I could think of were my superpowers. With my superstrength, I'd be able to check out as many heavy books from the library as I wanted, and I'd be able to carry them all myself. With my superspeed, I'd be able to clean my room in mere seconds (that is, if I could ever get the hang of not messing it up in mere seconds!). Maybe I'd even be able to do my homework at superspeed. And who knew what else was in store for me? I felt a flutter of excitement in my stomach, thinking of all the possibilities. Maybe I'd be able to fly. Or maybe I *would* have X-ray vision.

Of course, X-ray vision could turn out to be a problem. It would be useful for peering through cement walls to see if criminals might be hiding behind them, but in everyday life, it might be embarrassing. What if, like my speed, I couldn't control my X-ray eyes at first? What if I wound up accidentally seeing through people's clothes? I shuddered. Not even a superhero could handle seeing a school full of kids and teachers in their underwear!

When the end-of-the-day bell finally rang, I sprang to my feet.

I couldn't wait to get to Grandpa's store—I was hoping he'd be able to answer some of these questions!

After school, I waited for Dad to come and pick me up in his unmarked car. It looked like every other car that came by Sweetbriar Middle School, but it had some extra features: a removable siren and back doors that could only be opened from the outside. I'd been sitting on the curb for almost fifteen minutes when I saw the car come around the corner toward school.

I waved as I headed for the car.

"Hi, kiddo," Dad called through the open window. "Sorry I'm late. I got stuck at a crime scene."

"Hi, Dad."

"Hey, Zoe. Wait up!"

I turned to see Howie Hunt galloping toward us, his shocking-purple backpack bouncing on his shoulders. "Hi, Detective Richards," he puffed when he reached the car. "Catch any bad guys today?"

"Only one or two, Howie," Dad said, "but the day is still young. Would you like a ride home?"

Before Howie could answer, I cleared my throat. "Actually,

Dad, I was wondering if you could drive me to Speedy Cleaners instead."

"I don't see why not," said Dad. "Is Grandpa expecting you?"

I nodded, and as much as I hated to do it, I gave him the same fib I'd used on Emily. "I'm a part-timer again."

"Let me just call Mom and let her know," said Dad, flipping open his cell phone.

I turned to Howie. "I thought you were reading Romeo's lines with Emily."

"I was going to, but I needed to leave early, so she decided to do Lady Macbeth's soliloquy instead. Ms. Willowby let me do my audition first so I could leave."

"Mom says to say hi to Grandpa," Dad said, shutting the phone. "Hop in."

"If you're heading downtown," said Howie, "would you mind dropping me at my grandpa's store?" Howie's grandpa Gil owned a flower shop three doors down from Speedy Cleaners.

"Not a problem," said my father.

Howie and I climbed into the backseat.

"Let's stick the siren on the roof and drive really fast," I suggested.

"I don't think so." Dad chuckled. "Honestly, what is it with you kids and speed? Going fast isn't everything it's cracked up to be, you know!"

Oh yeah? I thought.

Dad turned the car onto Exley Street, heading toward Sweetbriar's shopping district, which is located on quaint little Main Street. Besides Grandpa's cleaners and Gil Hunt's florist shop, there are several clothing boutiques, some shoe stores, a bank, a candy shop, and, of course, Connie's Cosmic Comic Shop.

"Are you helping out in the flower shop today?" I asked Howie.

He shook his head. "No, I'm just gonna stop in and say hi to Gramps before I go to Connie's."

"Oh, right," I replied, not really paying attention. I'd started thinking about the training session again. I'd worn my only other pair of sneakers, but I wasn't sure if they were any stronger than the ones I'd burned up the day before.

"I figured that's where you were headed," Howie went on. "For the signing."

"Oh." I tried to focus on the conversation. "What signing?"

"Electra Allbright is making a personal appearance today! She's signing copies of the latest issue, Lightning Girl number three hundred seventeen."

I swung my head around to face Howie and clutched his shoulders. "Did you say Electra Allbright?" I cried. "Here? In Sweetbriar?"

"Yup." Howie wriggled. "Didn't you see it in the *Gazette*?"

I shook my head.

"It was a last-minute thing. Electra just announced out of the blue that she'd be in Sweetbriar and would make an appearance; that's why Connie didn't get a chance to promote it." He looked down at my fingers grasping his shoulders, and he winced. "Um, could you please let go of me?"

I gasped and released him at once. I hoped I hadn't accidentally used my superstrength on him. "Sorry. Did I hurt you?"

"No, it's just that anyone could see us." Howie wrinkled his nose. "I mean, hanging around together is one thing. Touching is a whole different story."

I rolled my eyes. Howie could be so immature sometimes.

76

I have to meet Electra Allbright, I thought. *I just have to!*

As Dad passed the comic-book shop, I could see the long line of autograph seekers waiting in front.

"Good turnout," Howie observed.

Dad pulled up to the curb between Speedy's and Hunt's Florist and got out to open the back door for us.

"Tell Grandpa I say hi," he said as I climbed out of the back-seat behind Howie.

"Sure thing," I said, closing the door quickly to avoid the customary long lecture about being careful, coming straight home, not changing plans without calling first, and all the rest of it. Dad waved and drove off.

Howie's grandfather was standing outside the flower shop. He was holding a handful of beautiful pink tulips, trimming the long stems.

"Hi, Gramps," said Howie, waving.

"Hi, Mr. Hunt." I gave him a big smile.

Mr. Hunt gave me his usual grumpy nod. Even though I was used to his bad temper, I was a bit taken aback. He seemed to be glaring at me even harder than he ordinarily did.

"Howie," I whispered, "do I have something gross hanging out of my nose?"

Howie shook his head.

"Then why is your grandfather staring at me?"

Howie shrugged, and I watched in surprise as Mr. Hunt angrily snipped the head off the biggest, prettiest tulip. The petals fluttered down to the sidewalk.

Three doors down the block, Grandpa Zack poked his head out the door of the dry-cleaning store. "Zoe, let's go!" he called, then nodded to Howie.

Howie waved.

Grandpa greeted Gil with a friendly "G'day, Hunt."

Mr. Hunt narrowed his eyes. "Richards."

"See ya later, Howie," I said. Eager to get away from Howie's grandpa, I turned and hurried toward the dry-cleaning store.

I could feel Mr. Hunt's piercing gaze on me all the way.

CHAPTER 10

"CAN I go to Connie's Cosmic when we're done?" I asked. "Electra Allbright is signing autographs."

Grandpa made a "hmmph" sound. "We'll see." He lowered his voice. "Did you recite the Pledge of Secrecy?"

I gave him a little salute, snapping my heels together. "Yes, sir."

"Excellent. And did you read about the peculiar tendencies of superpowers during the apprentice phase?"

I nodded. "Not only did I read about it, I experienced it first-hand."

"Ah. So they got away from you already, did they?" Grandpa tried to hide a smile. "Did you do any significant damage?"

"Not unless you count getting a tardy slip and having to do a spelling quiz at lunchtime. I trashed my closet, and Mom made me straighten up before I left for school, so I was late." I looked down at my feet. "D'you think these sneakers are going to melt

79

like the others? Mom will flip if I go home in my socks again."

Grandpa's eyes lit up. "I have something here that might work." He reached below the counter and pulled out a shoe box.

I gulped. "Er, is it supposed to glow like that?"

Grandpa just grinned and handed me the box. I opened it carefully. Inside were the most amazing sneakers I'd ever seen in my life. They were sleekly shaped and powerful-looking, and best of all, they were bright pink with two electric green stripes skidding along the sides.

"Official superhero cross-trainers, designed and produced especially for you," he declared.

"Wow! Thanks."

"I notified the Federation last night and they shipped them out right away."

"That was fast," I said, taking the sneakers out of the box to admire them. "I guess the Federation has its own top-secret, extrasuper, ultrapowered delivery service, huh?"

"Actually," said Grandpa, "we use FedEx."

He turned the sign on the door to CLOSED and let me move the hands on the little plastic WILL RETURN AT: clock to four-thirty. Then I put the sneakers on—they were a perfect fit, which was a relief because I wasn't sure how the Federation felt about returns—and followed Grandpa out back. The lot was empty except for a huge boulder in one corner and an ancient oak tree dead center. A tall wooden fence enclosed the lot on three sides, and the back of the dry-cleaning store blocked the fourth side. We were completely hidden.

"Okay," I said, rubbing my hands together in anticipation. "How fast do you want me to run? I was thinking we could start off by trying to break the sound barrier."

80

Grandpa laughed. "I like your enthusiasm. But today we're going to work on something a little different."

"Strength?" I guessed. "You want me to lift up a few of your industrial-sized clothes dryers so you can sweep behind them?"

"Thanks, but no."

"Well, what, then? How am I going to practice using my powers?"

"You're going to practice *not* using them," he said patiently.

"I don't get it."

"You read the part in the manual about apprentices not using their powers until they've passed the first exam, didn't you?"

"Yes, but—"

"And this morning you found out the hard way that your powers sometimes have a mind of their own, right?"

"Uh-huh."

"So, until you've progressed far enough in your training to take the primary test, your greatest challenge isn't going to be *using* your powers, it's going to be *not* using them."

I had to admit, that did make sense. And I didn't want to have to clean up a supersized mess in my room every morning. But it still seemed a bit unfair, like having the best birthday present ever and not being able to take it out of its wrapping.

The more I thought about it, the crummier it seemed. It was a bummer. It stank!

"All right," I said, trying to hide my disappointment.

"As you've already discovered, your superspeed can kick in anytime, without any say-so from you. At this point in your superhero development, your mind hasn't caught up to your body's abilities. Soon you'll be able to use your powers only when you choose to, but for the time being, you're going to

81

have to learn to control them when they sneak up on you." He pulled an empty crate from a pile by the back door and sat on it. "Now, think back to this morning. Did you have any sense that your speed was about to take over? Did you feel anything?"

"I felt this really intense tingling in my toes, then it moved up my feet, then—zoom!"

"What happened just before the tingling began?"

"I dropped my toast, and I knew I was going to be late for school." I remembered how anxious I'd been to get there on time, and I smiled, suddenly understanding. "Oh, I get it. I did think about how my superspeed would be useful to get me to school on time. It's like an instinct. When I need speed, speed shows up."

"Precisely," said Grandpa, sounding pleased that I'd figured it out. "But until the Federation okays it, you're going to have to learn to hang on to that natural reaction and slow yourself down." He gave me a serious look. "It's not easy. It's almost impossible to stop the superadrenaline from turning on the power when your body senses that you need it."

"Bummer."

"Yes." Grandpa cracked his knuckles. "Based on what you read last night, when a situation occurs that makes you feel like using your powers, what should you do first?"

I beamed at him because I knew the answer. "Like any good citizen, I call 911 and alert the proper authorities."

"Correct."

"Then what?"

"Then you do the most difficult thing you've ever done in your life." He shrugged. "You stand still."

82

Stand still. Right. How hard could it be?

"Okay," said Grandpa, "I want you to think back to this morning and imagine how it felt to get that tardy slip. Now think how you'd feel if you were about to get another tardy slip, even though you were only a couple of minutes from class."

I closed my eyes and pictured it. It was twenty-nine minutes past eight, and I was at the end of the schoolyard. The home-room bell was about to ring. . . .

"Feel anything?" he prompted.

I did. I felt the tingle again—in my toes, vibrating up through my calf muscles and into my knees. And suddenly . . .

I wanted to run so badly that I thought I might explode into a million pieces and there'd be nothing left of me but my awe-some new sneakers!

"Grandpa!" I gasped, reaching out for him.

"Steady, girl," he said. He stepped away from my arm. "Concentrate. Don't let the speed take over. Rein it in."

Rein it in? What did he think I was, a rodeo cowboy?

"I need to run!"

"Fight it. Control it."

"Tell that to my feet!"

Then I was off, speeding to the opposite side of the lot. I was heading straight for the fence!

"UH-OH!"

I could feel my heels digging in as I fought to drag myself to a halt, kicking up pebbles and carving out two deep ruts in the hard-packed dirt.

Stop, stop, stop, I told myself. *STOP!*

I slowed down. But I didn't stop.

"Better!" Grandpa called in an encouraging tone. "Keep going, just like that."

But "better" apparently wasn't good enough.

I figure I was going about eighty-five miles an hour when I hit the fence.

CHAPTER 11

LUCKY for me, I had that whole indestructible thing going on.

Too bad the same could not be said for the fence.

I heard a thud as I crashed into the thick wooden planks, followed by a series of creaking, splintering sounds.

"Zoe!" cried Grandpa, rushing across the lot.

For a moment, I was too dazed to move; I just stayed there, slumped against the fence. When Grandpa reached me, he took my arm and gently pulled me away from the wreckage.

"Ouch," I said, just for the heck of it.

Grandpa laughed. "Oh, c'mon now," he said, ruffling my hair. "You didn't feel a thing. You made quite an impression on the fence, though."

I looked at the fence. I'd left a pretty hefty dent; it was a perfect head-to-toe silhouette of me. "Cool. It's my outline."

"Yes," said Grandpa. "An uncanny likeness."

I giggled, then turned serious. "But I couldn't fight the power."

"It was only your first try," said Grandpa.

"I guess that means there's going to be a second try?"

Grandpa nodded. "And a third. And a fourth, and a fifth . . ."

"I get it," I said, sighing. "Until I do it right, right?"

"Right."

So much for getting Electra Allbright's autograph. How ironic was that? I couldn't go hang out with my favorite super-hero-comic-book author because I was too busy learning how to be a real live superhero. I grinned to myself. This was way weirder than any of Electra's plots! Even with her imagination, she'd probably have a hard time believing what was happening to her number one fan right now.

Grandpa made me picture myself at the bottom of the school-yard again, and before I could even get as far as imagining what the bell would sound like, the tingling sent me running high-speed laps around the lot.

"Grab hold of something," Grandpa advised. "The boulder. Let it anchor you."

I veered toward the huge rock in the corner of the lot. Clamping my teeth together, I willed myself to slow down, which was actually easier than it had been the first time. As the rock zoomed closer, I stuck out one arm, a bit like I was hailing a cab.

"Like this?" I called.

"Excellent," said Grandpa.

When I caught the rock, I stopped moving, but the rough surface of the enormous stone snagged my T-shirt, pulling a long, jagged tear down the side of it. I winced, then realized I didn't have to. When I glanced down, skidding, I could see there wasn't a mark on my skin.

I was still tingling, but the boulder was heavy enough—and my arm was strong enough—to keep me in one place long enough to focus all my energy on *not* running. I concentrated hard, and after a few moments, the need to run faded away.

Cautiously I let go of the boulder.

"Great job," said Grandpa. "Walk back toward me."

I felt a little wobbly, but I took a step. Then another.

Then I broke into an extremely fast skip.

Grandpa laughed.

"At least I'm not running," I said, skipping in circles around the lot. When I neared the oak tree, I jumped for a low branch and grabbed it with both hands. I hung there for a minute, swinging back and forth like a monkey, feeling as if I were just a heartbeat away from being able to fly right over the rooftops.

Reality check. Superpowers do not necessarily include flight.

I let go and dropped to my feet in the dirt.

Walk, I said to myself. *Don't run. Don't skip. Walk.*

And I walked.

I walked all the way to Grandpa, who hugged me.

"That's my girl! I think we can call it a day."

"Thank goodness!" I felt surprisingly tired out for someone who had spent the last hour trying *not* to run.

I followed Grandpa through the rear entrance of the dry-cleaning shop. He went to the front door and turned the sign around. Speedy Cleaners was officially open for business.

I took off my supersneakers and was just putting my own shoes back on when the little bell on the front door jangled and in walked a tall, carefully styled woman. She seemed to be about Grandpa's age, but this was one lady who was not going to let herself go as she got older. Her hair was blond and cut in a sassy pixie style, and her makeup was perfect. Her eyes were done up in earth tones to bring out their brilliant blue color. I caught myself thinking that Emily would definitely approve.

"Hello, Zachary," said the woman in a melodious voice. "Long time no see." She pushed a bag of clothing across the counter.

"Hmm," said Grandpa, reaching out to take the bag. I thought I heard him mutter "Not long enough" under his breath, but I must have been mistaken. Grandpa was never impolite to his customers. Or to anyone, for that matter.

"I'm going to be in town for a couple of days and I need to have these dresses cleaned and pressed," the woman instructed. Her voice was as warm and friendly as if Grandpa had greeted her like a long-lost bowling buddy. "Light starch in the shirts, please. Oh, and the yellow slacks are in need of a button."

As Grandpa began punching the keys on the computerized register, I noticed that the woman was looking at me. I smiled. She smiled back, and the register buzzed and began printing out a receipt.

"They'll be ready Thursday, after three o'clock," Grandpa said.

"Perfect." The woman was still smiling at me. "Now, Zack, don't tell me this pretty little thing is your granddaughter?"

"Okay," said Grandpa, handing the lady her receipt. "I won't tell you."

"So this *is* your granddaughter. Joey, is it? Chloe?"

"Zoe."

"Ah, yes. Zoe." The woman held out her hand for me to shake. "So lovely to meet you. I'm Electra Allbright."

"Nice to meet—" I began automatically, but in the next second, my mouth dropped open. "Did you say that you're Electra Allbright?"

"Yes, I did."

"Oh, wow!" I shook Ms. Allbright's hand harder, then made myself stop before the excitement of the moment brought out my superstrength. "I'm a huge fan of yours. Lightning Girl is my favorite comic! I have every issue! Well, except for issue number one, of course. But all the rest. Even the special limited-edition one with the holographic cover! Grandpa, you never told me you knew Electra Allbright!"

Grandpa frowned. "Must have slipped my mind."

Electra looked me up and down. "I'll bet she takes after you, Zack."

"Thursday, three o'clock," Grandpa snapped.

"And don't forget to replace that button." She fluttered her eyelashes at Grandpa, then patted my head. "Zoe, I do hope I'll see you again soon."

"Yeah, me too!"

"Ta-ta, Zack."

Grandpa mumbled a good-bye.

When Electra was gone, I whirled to face my grandfather. "I can't believe it. The world's most excellent comic-book author was just here! In your store! With some dry cleaning! And she's coming back on Thursday! I can bring all my Lightning Girl comics to the store, even the hologram one, which is, like, totally a collector's item, and when she comes in, maybe she'll sign them for me. Do you think she'd mind? Because I don't want to bother her, but—"

I stopped my blabbering midsentence when Grandpa

90

suddenly took hold of my shoulders. He looked more serious than I'd ever seen him.

"You must always remember what I told you," he said, looking me straight in the eye, "about keeping your identity a secret." His words were whispered in a no-nonsense tone. "Do you understand, Zoe?"

"Sure," I said. "I understand."

I wanted to ask why he looked so worried all of a sudden, and why he'd acted so weird with Electra Allbright, come to think of it.

But something in his eyes told me this was not the time for questions.

CHAPTER 12

"I can't believe you met Electra Allbright," Emily said. I was really grateful for her sympathetic excitement. "I mean, that would be like me meeting Abercrombie and Fitch!"

I beamed. "It was pretty cool."

"What was she wearing? I bet she's totally cutting edge."

But before I could answer, the voice of Ms. Willowby, Sweetbriar Middle School's drama teacher, boomed across the auditorium, welcoming us. "Good afternoon, future stars of the stage," she said. "I want to thank you all for coming and to let you know that I am so, so excited to be directing this year's theatrical production."

Her words echoed through the auditorium, where the students sat waiting to hear who'd been cast in which parts. Emily had told me her speech as Lady Macbeth had gone pretty well. Emily had spilled red ink on her hands for extra effect and Ms. Willowby had been impressed, even though Lady Macbeth imagined the spots on her hands in Shakespeare's play. Shame that the ink looked like it was never going to wash off. Emily was keeping her fingers carefully curled up, as if she could go through the rest of her life with bright crimson palms without anyone noticing.

Onstage, Ms. Willowby was just hitting her stride. "As you know, our play is an adaptation of an original. Adapted by me, that is. It is, in my humble opinion, a story of great emotional depth, a piece rich with theatrical vision. It is the story of a prince and a princess who, against all odds, find true love."

Some of the boys groaned and poked their fingers into their mouths, pretending to gag.

"I hope you got the lead," I whispered to Emily. I knew this was totally the sort of part she had always imagined playing. And maybe no permanent ink would be involved this time.

"Ladies first," said Ms. Willowby, taking a clipboard from the piano bench. "The lead role of Princess Wilhelmina will be played by . . ."

Emily grabbed my arm.

". . . Emily Huang."

Emily let out a gleeful shriek.

"Way to go!" I cried.

Caitlin, who was sitting in the row behind us, leaned forward and gave Emily a big smile. "Congratulations, Emily. If it couldn't be me, I'm glad it's you."

"Thanks," said Emily, and I could tell she felt a little awkward.

"All that matters is what's best for the play," Caitlin went on cheerfully, then sat back again.

"I didn't know Caitlin tried out for the role of the princess, too," I whispered to Emily.

Emily nodded.

I glanced over my shoulder at Caitlin, who was staring straight ahead. To my surprise, her smile had vanished and her eyes were focused coldly on Ms. Willowby. *Whoa,* I thought as a shiver ran down my spine. *She must* really *want a part in this play.*

Allison Newkirk was given the second most important part—the princess's mother, Queen Hildegarde—and Vanessa Stemple was cast as the wicked fairy. Betsy Davis would be playing the pivotal role of the royal purple aardvark. I was beginning to have some serious concerns about Ms. Willowby's theatrical vision. But Allison, Vanessa, and Betsy seemed thrilled.

Ms. Willowby continued to read off the names of the lucky actresses who'd been cast as wood sprites, ladies-in-waiting, and dance-hall girls; Caitlin's part wasn't announced until the very end of the list.

"Scullery Maid Number Two," she said. "Caitlin Abbott."

Emily and I both turned to congratulate Caitlin. She was smiling, but there was something icy in her eyes. I couldn't blame her—if the play meant that much to her, Scullery Maid Number Two was hardly in the same league as the princess, or even the princess's mom.

"Now for the boys," said Ms. Willowby, consulting the clipboard. "Beginning with the male lead, the role of Prince Irving St. Ives, Princess Wilhelmina's handsome and mysterious love interest, goes to . . ."

I giggled when Emily squeezed her eyes shut and whispered, "Please let it be somebody gorgeous. Or at least someone with good fashion sense."

But when Ms. Willowby cried out, "Howie Hunt!" the crowd fell silent.

Slowly every head turned to face Howie, who was sitting far off to the side in the very last row. There was a look of disbelief on his face.

"Me?"

"Yes, you," said Ms. Willowby. "Moving on . . . the role of the dishonest King Beauregard, husband to Queen Hildegarde, goes to Josh Devlin."

I know it was silly, but I couldn't help feeling a sudden pang of jealousy for Allison Newkirk. Somehow I must have ended up staring straight at Josh Devlin as I was fighting these totally unworthy feelings, because I suddenly realized he was looking straight back at me. And grinning. As if he knew exactly what I was thinking. No way! I turned right around in my seat so Josh wouldn't be able to pull any other telepathic stunts.

While Ms. Willowby read out the rest of the boys' roles, I told Emily all about meeting Electra.

"I just wish I knew why Grandpa treated her so strangely," I finished with a sigh.

"Maybe it's a dry cleaner–dry cleanee issue," Emily guessed. "Like, maybe Electra forgets to empty the pockets of her blazers before she drops them off. Or maybe she's just one of those customers who always misplace their pickup tickets."

I shrugged. "Maybe. The weird thing is, I'd have known before now if she were a regular customer, from when I was helping out. I've never seen her in the store, but she and Grandpa definitely knew each other. I wonder how."

"Something to share?" called a voice.

I gulped and went bright red when I saw that Mr. Diaz had joined Ms. Willowby on the stage and was looking straight at me and Emily with his hands on his hips.

"Er, no, Mr. Diaz," I called back.

He nodded and began to explain that he would be overseeing the stage crew, which included me. I hoped Mr. Diaz didn't think I'd be a troublemaker, what with the tardy slip and now being caught talking when I should have been listening. Emily and Caitlin went off to join the other actors onstage, while I followed Mr. Diaz and the other crew members backstage to learn about scenery and lighting, hopefully looking as if there weren't anything more important in my head than being the best crew member.

The first rehearsal went more smoothly than anyone had hoped—including me, given Ms. Willowby's unusual casting decisions.

Emily and Howie, surprisingly enough, had great chemistry, King Josh was smooth and confident (as if he'd be anything but brilliant!), and to my astonishment, Betsy Davis was utterly believable in her role as the purple aardvark.

Best of all, the crew schedule was going to be very flexible. I'd have plenty of time to practice using my superhero skills. Well, I would once Grandpa said I'd had enough practice *not* using them.

The stage crew's first job was to paint the backdrop. It was going to show the outside of a beautiful castle with rosebushes growing up a trellis toward Princess Wilhelmina's window. While the lead actors ran through their lines onstage, we were expected to paint and be generally creative in the wings without making a sound.

Mr. Diaz had spread newspaper on the floor to protect it from paint drips and splotches. He handed me a bottle of crimson paint and a narrow brush. "How are you at roses?" he asked.

"I'll do my best." I knelt down beside the blank canvas and was just about to paint the first flower when I noticed a headline in the newspaper Mr. Diaz had laid out.

THIRD JEWELRY STORE ROBBED THIS WEEK. SHIPMENT OF DIAMONDS STOLEN.

I'd heard a bit about this from my dad, but he tends not to talk about work stuff, which makes me wonder if he has police rules about secrecy that are like the superhero rules. Of course, instead of being Ordinaries, Mom and I are civilians.

Reading on, I learned that the Sweetbriar Police Department was baffled by the thief's method. All the jewelry stores had highly sophisticated security systems, but the robber had managed to get in and out without tripping the alarms. The article dubbed the crook the Slink. I guessed some editor was very proud of that.

I shuddered and tried to force the creepy story out of my head by concentrating on painting a perfect rose. Still, I couldn't help picturing some scrawny thief squeezing under doors all over Sweetbriar, like a very flexible cat.

The worst part was that in the last robbery, a security guard had been injured. He'd surprised the intruder and gotten a conk on the head for his trouble. When the guard came to, he couldn't remember a thing about what the Slink looked like, so the police still had no description. The article implied that the guard had been lucky that the Slink was in a hurry, or else the injury might have been worse. Much worse.

I felt another shiver go down my spine, then turned the newspaper page over and kept painting.

After rehearsal, I waited alone for my dad to pick me up. Emily's mom had picked her up promptly at five o'clock for their manicure appointment, and most of the other kids had gone down the street to hang out at the video arcade. I knew my parents would freak if I wandered so much as an inch off school grounds, so I stayed on the front steps. I could have called to let them know that I'd changed my plans, but it didn't seem worth the effort since I needed a lift home, anyway. *They'd never worry about me again if they only knew what I'm capable of,* I thought. *Well, what I'm going to be capable of eventually. It's going to be awesome!*

"It's going to be awesome!"

"Sorry?" I gasped, looking up.

Caitlin was coming down the steps, carrying her scullery maid costume. "The play," she said. "It's going to be awesome."

"Definitely," I agreed.

"And you did a great job on those roses!"

"Thanks."

"I just wish Ms. Foster could have found me a costume that fits," she said. "My sleeves are, like, ten miles too long."

"Maybe your aunt Nina can hem them for you tonight?" I suggested.

"My aunt works nights," Caitlin said absently.

"Teaching yoga?"

An odd look crossed Caitlin's face, but she just said, "Yeah, she teaches a lot of evening classes." A moment later, a black convertible shrieked up to the curb. In the driver's seat was Caitlin's aunt Nina, wearing big round sunglasses and a shimmery white kerchief, and looking more like a movie star than someone's aunt.

"Gotta go," said Caitlin, bounding down the steps. "See you tomorrow."

After the convertible sped off, I let my gaze wander to the park across the street. A little red-haired boy was playing marbles and slurping an ice cream cone while a woman who looked as if she might be his grandmother sat on a bench beside the large and rather ugly marble fountain. Her purse was lying beside her with a ball of wool, a handkerchief, and a wallet spilling out of it. Apart from them, the park was deserted, which was why a sudden movement and a flash of color near the fountain caught my eye.

A tall man was walking toward them. As he walked, he kept glancing over his shoulder, then to his right, then left.

And that's when my toes started to prickle.

"Uh-oh."

What had Grandpa said about a hero's inherent need to do good? About superintuition sending out signals when a hero senses danger?

My feet were really throbbing now!

I sprang off the school steps, dashed for the pay phone on the sidewalk, and punched in those three important numbers.

"Nine-one-one Emergency," came the operator's voice.

I could feel my feet quivering in my shoes as I clung to the phone. "I think there's about to be a crime committed," I said into the mouthpiece. "On the east lawn of Sweetbriar Memorial Park. There's a guy who—"

"What is your name, please?"

What the heck difference did it make what my name was?

99

How was an apprentice superhero supposed to maintain her secret identity if 911 operators needed to know her name?

"Uh . . . it's Lightning Girl," I lied.

The suspicious-looking guy was edging closer and closer to the woman on the bench.

"I beg your pardon?" said the operator; she sounded wary, as if maybe she thought this was a prank. "Did you say your name was *Lightning Girl?*"

"Um, no . . . I said Lila. My name is Lila. Lila . . . Pearl."

My feet began to twitch. The guy was reaching for the old woman's purse.

"Hurry!" I yelled into the phone. "Memorial Park. East lawn."

That was when the old lady shrieked. She sounded so terrified that I suddenly didn't care about the rules. There was no way the police would get there in time to stop him. I couldn't just stand there and watch! I had superspeed—and I was going to use it!

I lit out at full speed across the street just as the man closed his hand around the woman's purse.

He took off at a pretty good clip. The woman jumped up from the bench and screamed for help. I reached the bench in no time and, remembering what I'd done with the rock, flung out my arms to grab hold of it. Luckily, it was bolted to a metal plate in the sidewalk, and it stopped me from zooming on—for the moment.

"Are you all right?" I gasped to the woman.

"My purse!" she cried. "He stole my purse."

"The police are on their way," I told her.

I looked down and saw that my feet were still running. At this rate, I'd wear a hole all the way to China. I felt the bench wobble as I clung to it. Even as I sent up a silent wish that this would not be the moment my superstrength decided to switch on, I knew what was going to happen. And even though I was breaking one rule already, I didn't want to blow my whole secret identity on my very first attempt at crime-busting.

"You should probably get out of the park," I told the lady, thinking at superspeed, too, "in case that guy has a partner."

The lady didn't need to be told twice. She took her grandson by the hand and made a fast exit.

I let go of the bench and took off like a comet. *Yes!* The air rushed by me and the world was a blur.

I could see the purse snatcher up ahead; he'd reached the pond, about fifty yards away. I could hear police sirens drawing near, but I kept running. After all, it was what I was born to do.

I ran and ran. I was closing in on the guy now, and every part of me wanted to reach out, grab him by the collar, and turn him in to the cops. So what if I wasn't authorized to apprehend criminals yet? Maybe I'd get some kind of superhero demerit, but I truly believed in my heart that it would be worth it. This guy was a creep and he didn't deserve to get away.

In a split second I was beside the purse snatcher. I kept level with him for about three strides. He looked so shocked at seeing a twelve-year-old girl moving like a turbojet that I almost laughed. I reached out, ready to take hold of him . . .

And blew straight past him like a hurricane wind!

Not exactly what I'd planned to do.

Back up. Slow down! I said to myself.

But in spite of my heroic intentions, I was lacking one very important thing: experience.

I didn't know *how* to slow down! I was pretty certain the trick was to concentrate on my feet—same as getting them to move at superspeed. But concentrating on anything when you're moving at the speed of sound isn't easy!

I glanced over my shoulder. The thief was so shocked that he stopped in his tracks.

I kept going forward, straight toward the jungle gym on the other side of the park! Knowing there was absolutely no way I was going to stop in time, and not wanting to test my indestructibility on a solid steel frame, I jumped up and wrapped my hands around the highest bar, hoping that would stop me.

Instead the momentum took me spinning in circles over the bar. My stretched-out body sliced through the air as I went around and around and around like an Olympic gymnast.

Whoompf, whoompf, whoompf.

One more spin and I'd puke, I just knew it. Summoning my courage, I let go of the bar and soared across the grass about twelve feet above the ground. I landed in the pond with a huge splash and watched a small yellow fish arc through the air beside me. Luckily, it came back down in the water, looking rather surprised.

The thief was staring at me in total astonishment. As the police sirens screamed right into the park, he suddenly seemed to remember that he was about to be in big trouble, but it was too late.

The cops leaped out of their car, leaving their doors open just the way they do in the movies, and sprinted over to the purse snatcher, whom they quickly tackled and handcuffed.

Since there was nothing left for me to do, I waded out of the pond and headed back to school, my sneakers squishing all the way.

"Why are you wet?" Dad asked as I climbed into his car five minutes later.

"Um . . . well, it's part of the stage crew initiation. They take you to the locker room and throw you in the showers. I think it's an old theater custom." I forced a chuckle as my dad made some comment about those crazy drama types.

But I wasn't in the mood to laugh.

I felt miserable. I'd been a complete klutz back there in the park. From the bench to the jungle gym to the pond, it had been one stupid slipup after another. So what would happen when I did get permission from the Superhero Federation to stop purse snatchers and other bad guys? Would I be able to pull it off, or would I just turn out to be a Superklutz again?

And that was if they gave me permission at all, after I'd broken the number one rule about apprentices not using their superpowers in public.

"You okay?" Dad asked, studying me in the rearview mirror.

"Sure," I said glumly. "I'm . . . super."

But to be perfectly honest, I was beginning to think maybe I'd never be Super at all.

13

SUPERHERO TRAINING MANUAL
Book One
Chapter One Review:
Practice Test

The most effective way to stop a smoldering volcano from erupting is to:

a. gather nearby villagers to perform a ceremonial stop-the-volcano-from-erupting dance.

b. remove a medium-sized iceberg from the Arctic Ocean and drop it into the mouth of the volcano.

c. tunnel into the earth to create a drainage

passage below the volcano; this will funnel the lava downward instead of up.

A superhero can reverse time by flying around the planet backward at super-speed, but not during a leap year. TRUE or FALSE?

When tailing a villain, it is best to use:
a. a really fast vehicle.
b. the power of invisibility.
c. comfortable shoes.
d. all of the above.

It was way after midnight, and I was hidden beneath my comforter, studying the training manual by flashlight. But my heart wasn't in it.

The whole purse-snatcher thing had really left me feeling icky. I knew that as an apprentice I wasn't supposed to apprehend criminals yet, but I wondered—if I *had* been trying to nab him, could I have done it? Or would I have miscalculated my speed and overshot the target? I'd been a complete failure at *not* using my powers. What made me think I'd ever get the hang of using them?

I heard a car in the driveway and knew that Dad was finally

home. During dinner, he'd been called to a crime scene. That had been hours earlier. I tucked the training manual under my pillow and went downstairs. I met Dad just as he was coming through the kitchen door. His tie was loose around his neck, his badge was still clipped to his breast pocket, and he was holding a file folder under his arm.

"What are you doing still up?" he asked, smiling. It was a tired smile.

"Studying," I answered honestly. "I've got a big test coming up."

"Mom asleep?"

"Doubt it. She doesn't even close her eyes until she hears you come through the door." I watched him toss the folder onto the kitchen table. "So what kind of crime was it today? Assault? Murder? Kidnapping?"

"Robbery," said Dad. "Dexter's Diamond Depot." He opened the fridge and took out the milk carton.

"I'll get the Oreos," I offered, heading for the pantry. When I joined him at the table, he had already poured two glasses of milk and was spreading the contents of the folder over the table. I sat down and let my eyes wander over the pages of notes.

"This jewel thief business is a real puzzle," he said, dropping into a chair and helping himself to a cookie.

"I saw a headline. Aren't they calling the guy Stinky, or Slinky, or something like that?"

"The Slink," Dad corrected. "And it fits." He munched his cookie thoughtfully. "Seems like nobody can catch this guy."

"But that was before *you* were on the case," I said confidently. "Now that you're handling the investigation, things will be different."

107

Dad raised his eyebrows. "You make it sound like it's a sure thing."

"Well, it is." I swallowed a mouthful of Oreo. "You're a terrific cop. A great detective." I took a long gulp of my milk. "I bet you found all kinds of clues tonight."

"Actually, I didn't find any."

This surprised me. "None?

"I checked every door, every window, but there was no sign of forced entry and the alarm was never tripped." Dad shook his head. "This is one careful crook."

I frowned. "So what are you going to do?"

"I'm going to do what I always do in this kind of situation," said Dad. "Apart from coming home and eating milk and cookies, I'm going to keep trying. I'll go back to the crime scene and check everything all over again. Then I'll canvass the area and see if I can find someone who saw something or heard something. I'll ask questions. I'll keep looking."

I was confused. "But you said this Slink person was a careful crook."

"He is. Or maybe it's a she, who knows? No gender discrimination in the Sweetbriar Police Department!" He handed me another cookie and grinned. "But I happen to be a very careful cop."

"Oh." I put the cookie down on the table and looked at him. "But don't you ever get discouraged? I mean, you were at Dexter's Diamond Depot all night and you didn't find anything." I remembered how stupid and ashamed I'd felt in the park earlier that afternoon. "If I were you, I think I'd want to give up."

Dad crooked an eyebrow at me. "You think so?" He leaned forward and rested his elbows on the table to look me straight in the eye. "You think you'd just give up on something so important? Knowing that if you did, innocent people could become victims? That doesn't sound like you, Zoe."

All I could think about was how I'd struggled to keep from running, how I'd nearly torn up the bench, how I must have looked like some crazed chimpanzee swinging on the jungle gym. "But I tried—I mean, *you* tried. And it's not easy! It's hard. It's scary."

Dad nodded. "Yes, it can be very hard. But when I decided to become a police officer, I accepted the responsibility that goes with the job."

"What if you hadn't decided?" I asked, hoping I only sounded curious and not desperate, which was how I felt. "What if somebody had just come along one day and said, 'Hey, you. You're a detective, now go . . . detect.' Even if you'd never done anything like that before."

Dad laughed. "Well, I suppose that would make a difference."

"So let's pretend that's what happened," I said.

"Then I guess I'd make the best of it. I'd take into account how important being a detective was—after all, the job wouldn't exist if there weren't a need for it, right?—and then I'd put my mind to it and do it well. And I think eventually I'd realize that being chosen to serve my community, to help people, is actually a privilege."

I studied his eyes. They were serious, the way Grandpa Zack's were the night he told me about my superpowers. "You wouldn't quit?"

Dad shook his head. "Never."

We were quiet for a moment. Then I threw my arms around his neck and gave him a long hug. "You're the best, Dad."

109

"Thanks. I try. And good luck with your test. I know you'll do your best."

"Thanks, Dad."

Of course, he didn't know what I was talking about, not really. But it didn't matter. He'd made me feel better, just the way dads are supposed to. Even dads whose daughters are secretly training to be superheroes.

A few days later, Howie Hunt became my steady boyfriend, my first big love.

Yeah, right! That was about as likely as Emily wearing brown and purple together.

But unfortunately, that was how my mom chose to interpret the situation, and I had no choice but to go along with it, if I wanted to get in any more training sessions at the dry-cleaning shop.

I came barreling down the school steps after play rehearsal, and found my mother waiting for me on the sidewalk. Howie was right behind me. He was telling me that the scenery for the play looked great.

Mom smiled at me in that goofy way moms smile when they see you talking to a boy. I should have known right then and there where the whole thing was going. Mom had always talked about how cute it would be if Howie and I got married one day. Personally, I thought it would be a whole lot cuter if I married Josh Devlin!

"Hi, Zoe."

"Hi, Mom."

She turned her goofy smile to Howie. He blushed.

"What are you doing here, Mom? I told you I was walking to Speedy Cleaners after rehearsal, didn't I?"

"I'd rather drive you," she said. "With all this Slink trouble going on."

I rolled my eyes. "Mom, the Slink is a jewel thief. Why would he bother me?" I held up my wrist to show her the only bracelet I ever wore: a friendship bracelet made of blue and yellow string that Emily had given me. "I'm not exactly dripping with emeralds and rubies."

"Still," said Mom, "I'd prefer to drive you. Maybe Grandpa can use my help in the store, too."

This was a major problem. How was I supposed to train in secret with my mom hanging around?

"But it's such a nice day! I really kind of wanted to walk," I told her.

"I'm walking downtown, too," offered Howie, who had begun digging through his backpack.

"Oh, you *are*, are you?" Mom flashed another daft grin. "So you two were planning to walk downtown *together*?"

"Uh . . ." I shrugged. "Sure. I guess we might as well."

Mom hesitated. Her eyes shot from me to Howie, then back to me. Her grin was getting wider and more embarrassing by the second.

Suddenly Howie looked up from his backpack. "I forgot my math work sheet. I'll be right back." He galloped toward the school steps.

"Okay," said Mom in a singsong voice. "I get it."

"Get what?"

"You and Howie are . . . you know."

I didn't know. I gave her a funny look.

"You and Howie . . . He's your boyfriend, right?"

Wrong! Way wrong! I would have screamed it out loud if her statement hadn't sent me into shock. I just stood there with my mouth open.

Mom giggled. "You and Howie." She gave a little sigh. "That's so sweet."

Oh, no. Was she going to *cry*? "Mom, it's not what you think!"

She waved one hand in a dismissive gesture. "You don't have to be embarrassed, honey. I think it's really nice that you and Howie like each other."

Wait a minute. Was this the same woman who was so overprotective that when I started school, she followed the kindergarten bus in her car? The woman who insisted I leave the training wheels on my bike till I was nine? This didn't make sense! She wouldn't let me walk three feet ahead of her at the mall, but she was okay with me *dating*?

"I feel much better knowing Howie'll be walking right beside you," Mom said, getting back into the car. "He's such a nice boy." She gave me a dreamy look. "I suppose you and Howie will be walking downtown together all the time now."

I was just about to assure her that we wouldn't be doing any such thing when I realized that this was a perfect cover. Whenever I wanted to sneak off to train with Grandpa, all I had to do was tell my mother that Howie and I were going on a (gulp!) date. I crossed my fingers in my jacket pocket and reminded myself that the fib was for the good of my superhero training.

"Oh yeah," I said, hoping I wouldn't cough up my lunch. "All the time."

"Ask Grandpa Zack to drive you home in time for dinner,"

said Mom, starting the car. "Be careful crossing the busy streets, and have fun!"

When my "boyfriend" joined me on the sidewalk, we took off toward Main Street. As we walked, I had to keep reminding myself that serving the community and helping people was a privilege. But I couldn't help feeling that being a real-life superhero would never be as much fun as being a comic-book one. I mean, along with *her* secret identity, Lightning Girl got an underground cave dwelling, a supersonic space plane, and her own personal thundercloud. And with *my* secret identity, what did I get?

I got Howie Hunt as my fake boyfriend.

Well, I told myself, it could probably be a lot worse. I just couldn't imagine how.

CHAPTER

14

SUPERHERO TRAINING MANUAL
BOOK ONE
Chapter Four
Section 7 (d)

In this phase of development, an apprentice's superpowers are closely tied to his or her emotions. The fervor with which a power will assert itself is directly proportional to the feelings the apprentice experiences regarding the event or situation at hand. The stronger the apprentice hero's fear or concern for the potential victims, the more difficult it will be for said hero to harness his or her powers and keep them in check. It should be noted that positive emotions, such as joy, hope, and affection, can bring about the same result.

Two weeks later, my superhero training had really begun to pay off. I was getting faster and faster, and I couldn't believe how strong I was. Learning to control my strength was still the primary focus of my lessons. I was getting better at not letting the powers take over, but I still had to be careful.

Chapter Four of the manual explained that my emotions were at least partly to blame. This became clear to me when I opened the freezer to get some ice cream for hot fudge sundaes and accidentally lifted the entire refrigerator off the floor. (Well, ice cream *is* pretty important to me.) I put it down just a split second before my mother came into the kitchen to remind me that there were rainbow sprinkles in the cupboard as well. Knowing how excited I could get over ice cream, I figured it was lucky I didn't send the fridge flying right through the ceiling.

Being involved in the play was a nice break from thinking about or practicing anything remotely superpowered. I tried to avoid jobs like lugging heavy scenery and moving large props, on the chance that my superstrength would kick in accidentally. I stuck to the creative tasks and was really enjoying painting the scenery and making props.

On Friday afternoon, I was the first one to arrive at the auditorium, so I went to the lighting booth to turn on the house-lights. The booth was a small room with a huge window above the balcony opposite the stage; the lighting and sound people controlled everything from up there.

Through the window, I could see that some of the larger pieces of scenery were in place on the stage. The queen's throne was set at an angle stage left, and the princess's canopy bed was downstage. Even in the dim light I could see that the right side of the canopy was lopsided, and I made a mental note to adjust it later.

Suddenly I gasped. A small sinister-looking figure was hurrying down the center aisle toward the stage, carrying something long and pointy. I watched as the petite shadow climbed the stairs to the darkened stage.

I felt a surge of alarm rush through me, and true to my superhero powers, my first instinct was to leap from the window and stop the armed intruder. Maybe it was the Slink!

"Calm down," I told myself out loud. What would a jewel thief be doing here? The dressing rooms contained nothing more tempting than phony pearls and fake sapphires. It was probably just one of the actors, who'd turned up early to study lines. Or maybe one of the stage crew kids was checking the backdrop, to see if the paint had dried. If that was the case, some light would help.

I reached for the control panel and flipped a switch, and suddenly the stage was bathed in a brilliant glow.

And there, right in the middle, stood Caitlin Abbott, holding a huge pair of scissors. She froze midstep and squinted up toward the lighting booth. I guessed she was startled because she had a very strange expression on her face.

I flicked the switch for the loudspeaker. "Caitlin?" I asked, my voice echoing off the walls of the empty auditorium.

"Zoe? Is that you?" she called.

I turned off the spotlight that was blinding Caitlin, leaving only the houselights on. "Is everything all right?"

"Everything's fine." Caitlin hesitated, then smiled. "I suppose you're wondering what I'm doing with these scissors."

I hadn't been wondering, but now that she mentioned it. . . .

"Aren't they one of the props for the second act?" I said, recognizing the oversized pair of clippers. They were the ones the wicked fairy (Vanessa) was supposed to use to snip off the mustache of the king (Josh) in order to collect thirteen royal whiskers for a potion to turn the purple aardvark into an evil princess. It was definitely going to be an unusual piece of theater.

"Yes, they are." Caitlin nodded hard. "I was just using them to alter the sleeves of my costume, but I'm finished with them now."

I watched her scurry into the wings, and I chuckled. So much for spotting a dangerous criminal! I made a mental note to look up *superhero paranoia* in the training manual.

The rest of the cast and crew arrived, and I made my way backstage to find Emily.

She was studying her script with a frown.

"What's up?" I asked.

Emily shot me a look of frustration. "I'm trying to find my motivation in this scene. I just can't imagine why the queen would share her top-secret peanut butter cookie recipe with the prime minister when she knows perfectly well he's plotting to overthrow the monarchy."

"Well, keep working on it," I advised. "It'll come to you."

Emily went back to the script, and I headed for the prop table, where Josh Devlin seemed to be looking for something. He turned to me, and right away my heart thudded and I felt my cheeks turning pink. I told myself that no one could possibly have eyes that were really that piercing and that green.

"Hi, Zoe."

"Hi, Josh," I said, slightly impressed that I could speak.

"Have you seen the scissors?"

I tore my gaze away to look at the collection of props scattered across the table, though I doubt I could have found my own feet at that moment. I was talking to Josh Devlin!

Just then Caitlin came hurrying over, brandishing the scissors. "Here they are," she said, batting her eyelashes at Josh.

But Josh didn't even look at her as he thanked her. He was still looking at me. With a scowl, Caitlin dropped the scissors onto the prop table and walked away.

"So, Zoe . . . ," Josh said. "You painted the roses on the castle, huh?"

My toes were tingling and my knees felt sort of rubbery, but I couldn't tell if it was because my superspeed was about to kick in or because Josh's supersmile had kicked in.

"Roses," I said. "Yeah."

"They look terrific."

"Thanks." I gulped. "So. Save any rain forests lately?"

"Actually," said Josh, "I'm getting ready to start a letter-writing campaign to our congressman about cleaning up the Sweetbriar River."

"That's excellent." I picked up the scissors and handed them to him. *That's excellent?* I sounded like a great-grandmother! Any moment now, I'd pat him on the head. "Er, you were looking for these?"

"Yeah. Thanks. Ms. Willowby wants to block the mustache-cutting scene."

"Oh."

Josh took a deep breath. "Zoe, I was wondering—"

But before he could tell me exactly what he'd been wondering, Howie popped up beside me in search of his jewel-handled sword. He rummaged around on the prop table, sending an oversized tinfoil gauntlet rustling to the floor. "Hey, Zoe, we're walking downtown together after rehearsal again, right?"

"Huh?" (I was still sort of gazing at Josh, so it took me a minute to understand Howie's question.) "Oh. Yeah. Sure."

"I'll meet ya on the school steps then," said Howie, unearthing the sword and bearing it away in triumph.

Josh watched him leave. He looked a little surprised. And maybe disappointed.

"So Howie's walking you home?"

"Sort of," I said.

Josh was quiet for a moment. "Well, I'd better go find Vanessa. For the mustache cutting, you know."

"Okay." Feeling brave, I decided to try one of the cute gestures Emily's magazines were always recommending: I tilted my chin and gave my hair a little toss.

Unfortunately, it turned out to be a superpowered turbo hair toss, and the sweeping motion of my flowing locks created a gust of wind that toppled the prop table. Crowns, swords, and feather dusters all went crashing to the floor.

"Whoa!" said Josh. "What just happened?"

"Crossdraft." I gulped, bending quickly to clean up the mess. "Someone must have left the stage door open."

Looking sort of puzzled, Josh helped me pick up the table; then he took off with the scissors to find Ms. Willowby and Vanessa.

And I made yet another mental note: no more flirting.

CHAPTER 15

THE final rehearsal was going great.

The king and queen did their salsa dance number like a couple of pros, and when Betsy Davis sang her operatic solo, "I Am Purple, I Am Proud," we all knew we were going to have a hit on our hands.

I sat in the wings on the world's smallest and least comfortable stool, trying not to fidget as I waited for the next scene, which was a big one for Emily. It was the scene in which Princess Wilhelmina and Prince Irving announce their royal engagement, and the princess is so overjoyed that she breaks into song, another original written by Ms. Willowby, called "I'm Deserving of My Irving."

However, just before Emily's big number came Howie's conga-drum solo and tap-dance routine, which I had seen at least two hundred times. A large number of those times had been on the sidewalk as we walked to Main Street. I knew his steps even better than he did—and I still didn't feel like joining in as he swung, skipped, and tapped his way along six blocks and across two major intersections.

Peeking out from behind the heavy velvet curtain, I watched the scullery maids take their places as the backup dancers for Howie's routine. As usual, Caitlin was practically hidden by the conga drums. She always looked pretty miffed about being stuck back there, as if she actually *wanted* people to associate her with Howie's drum-and-tap sensation.

Today, I noticed, she didn't look miffed so much as . . . well, I wasn't sure. The word *smug* came to mind.

Mr. Diaz was helping the backstage crew set up the castle flats while Ms. Willowby cried out joyously from the orchestra pit that the scenery looked practically professional. I had to admit, it did look great. It was beautiful and solid, and played a pretty important role in the final scene when the prince courageously scaled the castle walls to rescue his princess. We'd spent most of the scenery budget on this, but Mr. Diaz said it would be worth it. Without the castle wall, the rose trellis, and the sturdy balcony, the final scene just wouldn't work. Not to mention that Prince Howie would risk serious injury in front of a packed auditorium. And nobody deserved to be injured, no matter how much they tap-danced in public.

I leaned back to admire my handiwork: the towering faux-stone walls covered in painted roses, the architectural turrets, and above them, the backdrop of night sky splattered with silvery stars.

Then something else caught my eye, something that was practically hidden by the giant cardboard cutout of the moon. One of the huge, heavy lights above the castle wall was swinging—

dangling, almost—as though it were about to fall.

But that didn't make sense. The day before, Mr. Diaz had climbed the scaffold to the catwalk and checked all the lights himself. He'd been absolutely confident that everything was ready for opening night. All the same, as I squinted upward into the shadows above the stage, I could see that the cord holding the big light was badly frayed. If it snapped, the enormous canister would drop and crush the castle! The play would be ruined! And even worse, someone could really get hurt! There was no way the castle would stand up to the force of that giant light falling on it.

I had to do something. A superhero would never abandon a friend in danger, rules or no rules. And nothing bad seemed to have happened since I'd chased the thief in the park—although maybe the Superhero Federation overlooked illegal uses of superpowers if the superhero turned out to be a klutz.

I shook my head. Whatever the rules said, my friends were in danger!

Maybe I could shinny up the curtain rope at superspeed, bolt across the catwalk, and catch the light before it fell. If I was fast enough, maybe no one would notice me. Of course, I didn't know how I'd be able to explain what I was doing standing on the catwalk holding a gigantic spotlight.

But I didn't have time to worry about that, not with Howie dancing his heart out right under the light.

I grabbed on to the heavy rope of the curtains, preparing to shinny, just as Howie went into his dance.

"The light!" I called out over the sound of Howie's frantic tapping. "The light's about to—"

"Keep dancing, Howie," Ms. Willowby hissed from the

123

orchestra pit. "What Zoe is trying to say is that the *lights* are *out*. The footlights. They should be lit for this scene." She turned and motioned to the tech people in the lighting booth. "Lights, please."

Overhead, the frayed cord was threatening to give way any second, destroying the scenery, and quite possibly squishing one of my friends.

"Which button is it?" called one of the lighting crew.

"I don't know. Try the third switch from the left," answered Ms. Willowby, smiling and bobbing her head along with the rhythm of Howie's tapping.

"Okay. Third one from the left—"

CLICK.

The auditorium went black.

Kids began to giggle and whisper in the dark, but Howie went right on dancing.

"Perhaps it's the second one," said Ms. Willowby. "Howie, Emily, dancers, please stay where you are. Don't move."

Good advice, but I wasn't about to follow it.

I called upon my superpower, and clutching the curtain rope, I tensed every muscle in my body and let the speed fill me from head to toe. My plan was to climb the rope.

I told myself to go up, toward the catwalk. But apparently vertical speed requires an entirely different sort of concentration from horizontal speed.

I took off at warp speed but in the wrong direction. Instead of upward, I was speeding across the stage. I was heading for the castle wall.

Luckily, in the blackout no one could see me.

Unluckily, in the blackout I couldn't see anyone, either. I guess night vision wasn't one of my powers.

But I could hear Howie, still tapping away. And I was heading straight for him! If we collided while I was going this fast, I would knock him out for sure—maybe even permanently. I had to stop before I ran over him like a bus. But as I should have learned from the purse-snatching incident, stopping wasn't exactly my best skill.

So I aimed for the place onstage where I had seen the lopsided canopy bed, and I reached out to wrap my right hand around one of the bedposts.

I must have misjudged slightly in the pitch-black, because instead of reaching the canopy bed, I went right past the edge of the castle backdrop. I reached out and managed to grab on to the edge, slowing down slightly. But only slightly. As I continued my superspeed skid across the stage, I could feel the castle, heavy as it was, getting dragged along with me! Just then my fingers slipped off the edge of the castle.

THWUMPF!

I hit the cushy velvet curtain that covered the back wall of the stage, which finally stopped me. Overhead, the rope snapped and I twisted my neck to see the shower of sparks as the enormous overhead light went crashing to the stage below.

Emily screamed.

Howie stopped dancing.

As quietly as I could, I untangled myself from the folds of the heavy velvet curtain and tiptoed through the darkness back to my stool in the wings.

Just as I sat down, the lights came back on.

"What happened?" Mr. Diaz called. "Is everyone okay?"

Everyone was, since the light had landed where the set had been. But in the orchestra pit, Ms. Willowby had slumped to the floor in a dead faint.

Mr. Diaz was staring at the castle backdrop, which, hav–ing *somehow* slid quite a long way toward the back of the stage, had been mysteriously saved from being flattened by the falling light fixture.

"How did *that* happen?" Emily gasped.

Mr. Diaz shook his head. "I have no idea." He glanced toward the wings and looked at me.

"Everyone okay?" he asked. There was a general murmur of "yes" from everyone in the auditorium. Mr. Diaz held my gaze for a moment, and he grinned.

I guess he was just glad that my beautiful roses were still intact.

Yes, that must have been it. I returned the grin.

Then Ms. Willowby came to and, as if nothing had happened, told Howie to take it from the top.

Rehearsal ran extra long. When Ms. Willowby finally dismissed us, everyone scrambled to leave, collecting their books and backpacks and heading for the exit. Not me. I waited around until everyone else had gone. Then I went back to the stage.

My footsteps echoed as I crossed into the wings. With a deep, steadying breath, I approached the ladder that led to the catwalk. I knew I'd be in huge trouble with Mr. Diaz if I got caught, but I just had to get a closer look at that rope. Maybe I'd inherited some of my dad's detective instincts after all.

I put my foot on the lowest rung and started the climb.

When I reached the catwalk, I walked carefully to the middle and leaned over the slim railing toward the cord that had once held the heavy metal light canister. I reached out and gave it a tug. It seemed strong enough. It wasn't old or worn out at all, apart from the end that dangled in the air, frayed as if something had chewed right through it.

So what made it break? A rappelling mouse? A hungry pigeon?

"Zoe?"

I looked down to see my grandfather climbing the stairs to the stage.

"Grandpa, what are you doing here?"

At the sound of my voice, he looked up. A bright smile lit up his face. "Zoe, did you fly up there?"

"No," I said, heading back toward the ladder. "I climbed up."

"Oh." Grandpa shrugged. "Too bad."

When I joined him on the stage, he gave me a hug. "You were supposed to be at the store at four o'clock," he reminded me. "I was worried something had happened."

I slumped into the queen's throne. "Something did." I told him all about the broken rope, the falling light, and Howie's near miss.

"No one saw you?"

I shook my head.

"Sounds like you had an exciting afternoon," he said.

"I just went up there and checked the rope," I told him. "I'm no expert, but it doesn't look as if it should have snapped." I frowned and stood up slowly. "Actually, it looks as if it was cut."

"Cut?" Grandpa raised his eyebrows.

"Yes, cut. On purpose. And whoever cut the rope made sure they picked a light that was directly above the scenery, as though they wanted to destroy it."

"But why?" asked Grandpa. "And who would do such a terrible thing? And when in the world would someone have the chance to climb up to the catwalk and fool with the equipment?"

Suddenly my eyes flew open and my heart dropped to my toes. "I saw one of the actors sneaking around in here before rehearsal—and she had a pair of scissors!"

"That does sound suspicious," Grandpa agreed. "But why would one of the actors want to ruin the play?"

Before I could make my best guess, the door at the rear of the auditorium slammed. I turned to see Caitlin and Emily coming down the aisle.

"Zoe!" cried Emily. "We've been waiting for you."

"You have?" I went down the stage steps and met them in the middle of the auditorium. Grandpa was right behind me.

"Howie's waiting, too, out on the front sidewalk," said Emily. "He told us you were walking downtown together, so we thought we'd go along with you. We were going to get some fries at the Burger Barn. I'm starving after that rehearsal!"

I glanced at Grandpa. "Well, I was supposed to go to the dry-cleaning store. . . . "

"Oh, don't worry about me," he said. "I'll just close up and go home early tonight."

"Mr. Richards," said Emily, "you do alterations at Speedy Cleaners, don't you?"

"We sure do," said Grandpa. "My wife's the best seamstress in Sweetbriar."

Emily turned to Caitlin. "I noticed just before the lights went out that the sleeves of your scullery maid costume aren't even. I bet if you bring it to Speedy Cleaners to be altered, it will be ready for opening night."

Caitlin smiled politely, but her eyes seemed stone cold. "Good idea," she said stiffly.

"Drop it by anytime," said Grandpa, and he started to tell Caitlin the store hours, but I wasn't really paying attention because I was remembering what Caitlin had said when I caught her with the scissors. She'd said she had already altered the sleeves on her costume.

Grandpa waved to me as he headed toward the exit. "See you tomorrow, Zoe. Have fun."

"Yeah," I replied vaguely.

"Earth to Zoe! Let's go," said Emily.

Without a word, I followed her and Caitlin out of the building to the front sidewalk, where we met Howie.

On the way downtown, Emily started chattering to Howie about how she thought he should try saying his lines with a British accent. I fell back a few steps and motioned for Caitlin to join me.

She looked at me with a sweet, curious expression.

"You told me you'd already altered the sleeves of your costume," I said. "That's why you had the scissors."

Caitlin blinked, but her expression didn't change. "Yes. That's what I told you."

"So you lied?"

For a moment, Caitlin was silent. "Yes, I lied."

I glared at her, wanting to shout, to accuse her of trying to ruin the play. My arms and legs tingled, but I think that this time it was just regular anger. Didn't she know she could have hurt someone badly?

But I didn't get the chance to shout at her because in the next second she was blurting out a confession.

"I tried to fix the sleeves myself," she said, her voice trembling. "But I made a huge mess of things. The left sleeve is way shorter than the right one." She looked as if she might burst into tears. "I was afraid I'd be in trouble with Ms. Willowby for ruining the costume. I'm going to bring it to your grandfather's store to get it fixed. I'll even pay for the tailoring with my own money."

Immediately a knot formed in my stomach. I'd almost accused her of doing something horrible—murderous, even—and now

I felt like a real jerk. "W-well," I stammered, "why didn't you just tell me that?"

She shrugged. "I was too embarrassed."

I started walking again, slowly. Her story made sense, and I wanted to believe her. I just wasn't sure I did.

Caitlin was smiling now. "Just promise me you won't tell anyone that I almost ruined my costume, okay?"

"I won't," I assured her.

Ahead of us, Emily had stopped coaching Howie on his accent; she turned and looked at us over her shoulder. "So did you get a look at Josh Devlin in his king costume?" she asked.

"I saw him talking to Zoe at the prop table," said Caitlin. "I think he likes her."

Emily let out a little yelp of joy. "Zoe! That would be the best thing in the world. You and Josh, like, falling in love and getting married."

Howie rolled his eyes. "Are we going to the Burger Barn or not?"

Caitlin let go of my arm and caught up to Emily. "Fries and sodas are on me," she said.

I didn't have a soda. Soda always makes me burp, and I was afraid that maybe even my burps would be superpowered. For all I knew, one good belch from a superhero could set off an earthquake or an avalanche. So I bought a lemonade (which I insisted on paying for myself) and joined Emily on the bench in front of the Burger Barn. Caitlin was still inside with Howie, waiting for the orders of fries while Howie tried to decide whether he wanted grape soda or root beer.

Emily started talking about the sweaters on sale in the boutique next door. I tried to listen, but I had a lot to think about, starting with Caitlin and the scissors. The fact that the rope had been cut was an awfully strange coincidence. I couldn't figure her out. She'd been really snotty when she interrupted me and Josh at the prop table, but when she told Emily that Josh might like me, she seemed happy for me.

It suddenly occurred to me now that Josh had never gotten around to asking me the question he'd wanted to ask when we were standing at the prop table. Maybe he'd ask me the next time I saw him.

And then there was the first superhero test looming. I had one more night to study. If I passed, I'd move up to the next level of apprenticeship. I wasn't sure what that involved in the way of training, but it had to be better than what I was doing now, which was a whole lot of nothing. Maybe in the next level I'd actually be allowed to *use* my powers. I wondered whether the little incident with the light would be held against me when it came time to move up a level. I hoped the fact that I'd saved the play—and Howie—would mean that I didn't get into too much trouble for unauthorized use of powers. This whole superhero thing was turning out to be more stressful than I could've imagined!

"Are you all right?" Emily asked.

"Hmm?"

"You seem kind of out of it."

I shrugged. "I've got some stuff on my mind."

Emily glanced back through the window. Howie was still dithering over the big root beer–grape soda debate. "He'll be in there forever," she predicted, taking her last swallow of soda and hopping

133

up from the bench. "Come on, I have an idea."

"What?"

"I'll tell Caitlin and Howie to meet us at Connie's Cosmic, and you can pick up the latest issue of Thunder Chick."

"Lightning Girl," I corrected.

"I know! I was just testing to see if you were listening!"

Emily went into the store to tell Caitlin we were going on ahead. Caitlin turned and smiled at me through the window.

Emily returned. "We're outta here."

"But you don't even like Connie's store," I said, getting up from the bench and following her to the corner.

"That's okay," said Emily. "You're my best friend and you look unhappy, so I want to cheer you up. I bet reading about Lightning Girl's superheroic adventures will take your mind off whatever's bothering you."

Bet it won't, I thought. But as we crossed the street and headed toward the comic shop, I knew how lucky I was to have a friend like Emily. I reached out and gave her hand a squeeze, hoping she could tell how grateful I was.

And then it hit me. Emily, my mom and dad, even Howie Hunt and Main Street, with all its friendly store owners and shoppers—*these* were the reasons I was a superhero! These good people and others like them all over the world needed to be looked after, protected, kept safe from villains and criminals and other horrible stuff!

And it was going to be my job—my privilege—to do it.

I finally understood, and I felt a swell of pride. And, yeah, *major* pressure, but suddenly I didn't mind so much about the pressure. I'd mess up again, I was pretty sure of it, and I'd get frustrated and tired and probably scared, too.

But my family, my friends, and millions of strangers *needed* me, and they needed the other superheroes, too.

Emily was holding open the door to Connie's shop. "Let's go. I can't wait to see what the forces of good and evil have in store for us!"

"Neither can I," I said. And I meant it.

ZOE QUINN lives in Maryland and still enjoys reading comic books. *The Caped Sixth Grader: Happy Birthday, Hero!* is her first novel.